THE
DIME
MUSEUM

ALSO BY JOYCE HINNEFELD

The Beauty of Their Youth: Stories

Stranger Here Below

In Hovering Flight

Tell Me Everything and Other Stories

THE
DIME
MUSEUM

Joyce Hinnefeld

Unbridled Books

This is a work of fiction. The names, characters, places and incidents are either the product of the author's imagination or are used fictitiously, and any resemblance to actual persons living or dead, business establishments, events, or locales is entirely coincidental.

Unbridled Books

Copyright © 2025 by Joyce Hinnefeld
"A Mind of Winter" appeared online at JMWW.

All rights reserved. This book, or parts thereof, may not be produced in any form without permission.

ISBN 978-1-60953-157-7

Book design by Jane Raese

*To my many and varied students
through the years, with gratitude
for the many and varied things
they've taught me*

Nothing matters but the quality
of the affection—
in the end—that has carved the trace in the mind
dove sta memoria
> —Ezra Pound, *The Pisan Cantos*

This song is for my foe,
the clean-shaven, gray-suited, gray patron
of Hartford, the emperor of whiteness
blue as a body made of snow.
> —Terrance Hayes, "Snow for Wallace Stevens"

Contents

BEFORE THE FLOOD

L'Acqua Alta
  VENICE, 2019 — 3

The Dime Museum
  CHICAGO, 1965 — 28

A Mind of Winter
  PHILADELPHIA, 2012 — 53

Winged Siren Seizing an Adolescent
  LISBON, 2020 — 63

PHILADELPHIA, APRIL 2020

Disembarkation Sickness — 91

Dreamers — 119

Indifferent History — 135

Tenderness — 143

CODA

Those Who Can
  PRAGUE, OCTOBER 2021 — 161

BEFORE THE FLOOD

L'Acqua Alta

VENICE, 2019

WHEN I GOT TO VENICE in the fall of 2019, I was thinking about death. This made me sort of a cliché, I knew that, and it wasn't the first time. I'm a twenty-first century white guy, I like basketball, and my name is Charlie, so I can't get out of bed in the morning without being predictable and banal. Which is a big part of the problem.

I thought about it in a sort of casual, twenty-first century way. Not at all like the novel (which I never finished), and also not like the film. Instead of cholera, I was thinking about suicide. Not about actually doing it; I was really too fortunate a person for that. It was more just a sort of general curiosity. Something to look up. Maybe, no definitely, I was bored, had been bored, really, for the past five years, since graduating from college.

I assumed a suicide would be by drowning in a place like Venice. Mostly people tried in the lagoon, though in the last ten years at least a couple people had thrown themselves into the Grand Canal from the Rialto Bridge. But when would a person do it? The Grand Canal was always clogged with boats, fast vaporettos and the airport Alilaguna boats, its countless gondolas. No privacy for a quiet plunge, not even in the middle of the night, as I knew from shuffling back from the bar near San Paolo where Geoffrey, my mother's most recent boyfriend, knew the owner and so I got mostly free drinks. The Grand Canal was teeming at all hours.

At the end of the small, dark street where I was staying I could have stepped right off the edge and into one of the narrower canals, the Rio di San Luca. My street was a *rio terra*—a filled-in former canal. Like every street in Venice, it had an interesting history. Once it was a known retreat for murderers, but now it ended at the front door of a palazzo housing a young arts collective that rented out some of the lavish rooms. Geoffrey had arranged this for me too, when I decided to head to Venice after bumming around Europe for most of the summer. He knew somebody on the art collective's board.

Geoffrey. Just the name tells you everything. He was the kind of guy my mother had dated for years. New money, and lots of it, but Geoffrey was Australian and had a sense of humor at least. That was a nice change.

At night I felt almost magnetically pulled to the end of the damp-smelling *rio terra*, to the lapping water of the narrow canal. But even there a singing gondolier or one playing an accordion passed by roughly every three minutes. Sometimes, lying in my bed in the early evening, I timed them. I knew a potential suicide wouldn't sink fast enough, and also not deep enough, in the Rio di San Luca.

A week or so after I arrived, I persuaded the owner of the tiny and crowded bookstore at the other end of the street to let me work there, basically for nothing. I didn't need money, I needed something to do. My limited Italian wasn't a liability. The only people who walked in were tourists, usually looking for postcards or games or James Patterson novels. They thought it was a kind of Barnes & Noble, but Tomasso, the owner, only sold art books and literature and contemporary Italian novels. The store had tons of those things, all stacked on high tables and spilling off shelves that reached to the ceiling.

I worked during Tomasso's extended lunch hour, from 1:30 to 5:30 each afternoon. It baffled him still, he said, that this was the time when American tourists chose to shop. It was an ordeal to stay open for the limited business he got until I came along, he said.

Basically, I was paid in books. I'd take a few back to the room where I was staying, because I had nothing there but a phone charger and a backpack full of t-shirts and shorts. I owned one pair of jeans, and it was autumn and turning colder, so soon I'd have to buy more. But for now, in late September, it was still reasonably warm. I used Tomasso's store as more of a lending library really. I'd take one stack of books back to my room one day and then, a few days later, return those and replace them with others. Henry James, because you're supposed to read him in Venice. Books about Caravaggio and Titian and Tintoretto. A biography of Vivaldi. Poetry by Louise Bogan and Adrienne Rich. I'd brought copies of *The Cantos* and Stevens's *Harmonium* along with me, so I added those and fanned everything out on the table at the end of my bed, in case I brought anyone back, which I sometimes did. I thought maybe that way we'd have something to talk about, but mostly, when we weren't having sex or sleeping, the women I brought back and I just looked at our phones.

I didn't actually read most of these books. But I read Bogan and Rich as obsessively as ever. I'd done that since college, when Min told me they were the poets she'd liked most in the one poetry class she took. I'd thought, then, that if I read them I might understand her, that these women she'd admired maybe held the key to Min. Apparently I still thought that.

"I'm really only interested in poetry by women," she announced to me one afternoon in February, early in our final semester at our small college in Pennsylvania. We were lying naked in my overheated room, on sheets I hadn't changed since sometime in the fall. I shared a big and nearly empty apartment in a crumbling old house on the edge of campus with three guys from the basketball team. They were hardly ever there, which was how I'd managed to get the one room with a radiator that actually worked, clicking and hissing and banging but at least also cranking out a steady stream of hot, dry air.

"These sheets are disgusting," Min said that day. "I'm taking them home to wash."

"I've told you, you can't do that. They're the only sheets I have, and I've got to put something between my body and this disgusting mattress."

"So use a towel or something," she said, curling her little body around mine and pushing out of my hand the book I'd grabbed moments before—thinking she was drifting off to sleep.

Min was a commuter; she lived with her mom, in Reading. Unlike me, she'd worked her ass off in high school to get into college and she still did. Min was a nursing major. I mostly smoked weed and played pick-up basketball. I hadn't made the team and so was done with practice and all that. Besides, I thought playing Division III college basketball served no real purpose. Kind of like my English major, my roommates liked to remind me.

That was one of two significant changes in me since high school: I'd discovered that I loved poetry. Reading it mostly, but writing it too, even sometimes performing what I wrote at open mics in bars. The second big change was falling in love with Min.

So I didn't really mind when she knocked the book out of my hand that day. I remember it was *Women in Love*, and from this distance I'm not sure which is more pathetic: that that's the book I was reading or that I still remember what it was.

Min's body was tight and strong but also lush. She was small, only a little over five feet tall—more than a foot shorter than me. But when she wrapped her arms around my waist, it felt like being drawn into the sweetest, gentlest wave. One that held you and rocked you, not one that knocked you down and then pounded you around. I'd been with a number of girls who were more like that by the time I met Min. I've been with even more since.

So what made me open my big mouth that day, when she knocked the book out of my hand, then kissed me and climbed on top of me, and then, later, told me it was stupid how I kept reading all those dead white guys? Why did it even *matter*? She'd taken one poetry class. One. The semester before, an intro course that met the fine arts requirement, and she took it with an adjunct that I knew all about—an older woman everyone loved. Everyone but the full-time English Department faculty. This teacher had angry opinions about Eliot's and Pound's anti-Semitism and Wallace Stevens's racism, about the sexism of pretty much all male poets. At least the older ones. Her students learned from her that this minimal, relatively simple reading they were doing was enough to qualify them as people who knew about, and understood, all the poetry that had ever been written.

Okay, I shared some of that professor's views. *Some* of them. I knew about hip hop and spoken word and genuinely respected both as art forms. But for some reason, that afternoon, in my Min-warmed bed—petty enough to be annoyed about possibly losing my sheets for a night—I decided I needed to set Min straight.

"Well, come on, Bogan and Rich are also dead," I said. "And they were white. And you know, really, taking that one class doesn't exactly make you an authority, or give you the right to criticize what I'm reading."

We'd been bickering more and more by then, about all kinds of things. The fact that on days when she had clinicals the only time when she could see me was during the late afternoon when I wanted to play basketball. The tight, low-cut tops she wore to class, which—I knew because how could you not?—made other guys gape at her, practically drooling.

Maybe it had all been building till then, and she was finally at her limit. Maybe that's why Min stared at me with a look on her face that I couldn't read, then pulled on her clothes and grabbed her things and said, "Keep your goddamn janky sheets," before giving D. H. Lawrence one last kick under the radiator and walking out the door.

I did wash the sheets at some point during that week when Min and I didn't speak or see each other, and I made the bed with my eyes closed, so as not to have to see the mattress. That was another thing that bugged Min: how squeamish I was. She might not know that much about literature, she told me often enough, but at least she could draw blood or change a bedpan without gagging.

* * *

ACQUA ALTA IS THE TERM used by tourists and other English speakers (who drop the Italian article) for recurring high waters in the Venetian lagoon—high tides from the Adriatic that have a domino effect and lead to flooding in the streets and plazas of Venice. Flooding that happens more frequently than ever, Tomasso says, thanks to climate change.

I learned a lot about *l'acqua alta* from Tomasso, whose bookstore is named *Prima dell'alluvione*. Before the Flood. Tourists think it's meant to be biblical, but "I am speaking about the present," Tomasso says. The shelves and tables are all high off the ground, unusually high, and each time the water rises high enough to seep into his shop Tomasso makes a mark on the wall by the door and notes the date. He sits on a stool at the store's high front counter. These are all gestures designed to remind people that things are getting worse, he says, though it's not clear his gestures are having any effect.

"Look at them," Tomasso said to me on the first of three days of *acqua alta*, a cold October day that made me want to curl up in the bed in my room in the palazzo and not come out until the rain ended. He was pointing at the groups of tourists, still there outside his shop window, still tramping along the narrow *rio terra* in plastic rain ponchos, with plastic bags tied around their boots.

"Nothing stops them. What kind of idiot wants to walk out of doors in something like this? But they've spent the money, they have the hotel room, they're here in Venezia for holiday and they're going out there, goddamn it, no matter what. No matter about the rain and the wind and the floods."

I thought he was a little hard on the tourists; I thought lots of people in Venice were, considering the fact that tourists were the source of their livelihoods. Though I also kind of thought he was right. All those people covered in all that plastic looked ridiculous. But the entire Venetian economy depended on them, so wooden walkways were erected, umbrellas and ponchos and cheap rubber galoshes were for sale outside all the *tabacchi*—more money to be made from tourism—and everyone continued with their sightseeing. Never mind that the Plaza San Marco was immersed in a couple feet of cold and reeking water.

Everyone made the best of it somehow, and that could have been inspiring. Like the Titian painting in the Accademia with sections cut out of the bottom to accommodate the doors into the gallery. That bothered me so much, and I couldn't say why.

Tomasso only shrugged about it, the consummate Venetian gesture.

"The painting's still there. The people still come."

I needed to be more like Tomasso probably. It was clear he also thought I needed to be more like him—that is, more like a middle-aged Italian man. He was constantly giving me advice, whether I asked for it or not.

Lots of people I met in Venice wanted to offer me advice. *What are you doing here?* they would ask, with the unspoken question being what are you doing here for so *long*, "working" (but not really) in a bookstore, drinking and smoking every night, often bringing home a different girl? Sometimes an American one, sometimes not.

"Is it a girl?" Tomasso asked me one day not long after I started working for him. And so I told him about Min. About how she'd said that our backgrounds were probably too different—me the son of divorced parents with more money than some small nation-states, Min the daughter of an undocumented woman from the Dominican Republic who'd cleaned hospital floors and hauled bags of medical waste so she could pay rent on their cramped apartment—even though I'd never seen those differences as such a big a deal. About how once Min had said that, before one of our frequent break-ups during the first couple years out of college, it seemed like I couldn't stop thinking about it. And I had lots of time to think about it, without a job, with Min working long shifts at a hospital in Philadelphia and refusing to let me move in with her. About how the more I thought about it, the more I couldn't figure out what to do. So I drank and smoked and cheated on Min to try to distract myself—always when we were broken up though, so arguably I wasn't cheating on her. Or so I told myself.

And time went by.

When my mother's new boyfriend told me he knew of a place I could stay in Venice for nothing—a room in a palazzo, as a matter of fact, one filled with an odd collection of contemporary art—I decided to head there next.

Rich people often don't pay for things. That's one of many things that Min couldn't stand. It's one of many things I can't stand about myself as well. There's a long, long list, which is why, some nights, I try to convince myself that the lagoon is calling to me.

Tomasso told me that the answer was to ask Min to marry me, and not take no for an answer.

"Get married," he said. "Trust me. Once you're married, she's there, you have each other, you can let everything else go." He patted his own belly. "You'll eat well, you'll sleep well, you'll have sex sometimes, when you both aren't too tired and you're both in the mood."

I looked at him, there on his stool behind the counter, glued to his computer screen. His skin had a sallow undertone, and he was balding but also needed a haircut. He had the belly that most middle-aged men have, except for the ones my mother dates. His glasses were about fifteen years out of date. I wouldn't have described Tomasso as a happy man.

And anyway, I *had* asked Min to marry me, more than once, and every time she'd told me no. I didn't exactly blame her. And I couldn't not take no for an answer (what Tomasso actually said was that I should refuse the response of no or something like that—in Italian—but I knew which overdone American phrase he was grasping for). What was I supposed to do, throw her over my shoulder and drag her to City Hall?

But it struck me, at that moment, that he might be right. That I could be content if Min married me, and I just ran a bookstore. Or if not content, certainly not suicidal.

Of course I wasn't really suicidal. People were still interesting to me, and so were books, and sometimes music and art. From what I've read I think you have to feel that nothing and no one is interesting to you anymore to be fully ready to pack it all in.

I was still intrigued by some of the people I met in Venice. Artists who displayed their work on the gallery level of the palazzo, for instance, and came to the openings that happened there every few weeks. They did a lot of things with neon, and a lot of sculptures depicting body parts, sometimes mangled. There was one woman, a painter, who always portrayed victims of drowning—old women, children, a dog. Realistic images in which they were all vaguely bluish, lying on the banks of the lagoon or on the Riva del Vin along the Grand Canal, bathed in bright sunlight. They looked somehow relieved to be dead.

Another artist I met, Stefan, was a musician—a violinist. I'd gone to hear the chamber orchestra he played with on several occasions, at concerts they did three nights a week in an old church near the Accademia bridge. Mostly Vivaldi, which, he said, is what the tourists wanted. He could play Vivaldi in his sleep, Stefan told me.

Part of what fascinated me about these concerts was the musicians' obvious contempt for their audience. At least they seemed contemptuous to me. Did no one else in the audience notice it? I'd performed a bit, at poetry open mics and in a lame band in high school, and I was pretty sure I could recognize scorn for an audience when I saw it. So one night I lingered afterwards, smoking at a side entrance to the church. When Stefan walked out, I was sure I saw him smirk in my direction.

"*Parla inglese?*" I asked, risking more contempt, but he only nodded, accepted the cigarette I offered him and said, "You come a lot. Wouldn't you rather hear good music, not just this drivel for tourists?"

I always thought the music I heard in the church was good. Predictable maybe, well-known, even to my untrained ear; there was always at least a concerto or two from *The Four Seasons* and these were, it seemed to me, beautifully performed. "To be honest," I said, "I'm not sure I'd be able to tell the difference."

Just offering Stefan a cigarette would not have been enough to interest him, I learned that night. He would never have joined me for a night of drinking then, and a number of nights after that, if he hadn't seen the book I was carrying— which was the paperback edition of Ezra Pound's *Cantos*.

I also saw him taking note of the sleeve on my right forearm, which seemed to confuse a lot of people. It was a detailed and realistic image of an owl, created by one of the more expensive tattoo artists in Philadelphia. People tended to form their own theories when they saw it, at bars or basketball games at the Y but especially, I'd discovered, in Europe. I hadn't grown a beard and I hadn't shaved my head; in fact my hair was long, for the first time in a while. But most young guys I talked to in Europe, and particularly in Italy, took one look at my ink, my blond hair and my blue eyes—not to mention the kinds of books I often carried around—and assumed one thing: CasaPound, the loose group of Mussolini-loving white boys cropping up all over Europe.

I'd begun to wonder about how often guys like Stefan seemed to find me, wonder if I was somehow making it happen, unconsciously. If in fact I was finding *them*. If I was, deep down, just a neo-fascist in waiting. Or worse, an American white supremacist. I had money I hadn't earned and more privilege than I knew what to do with—a stupid and ridiculous problem to have, but a problem nonetheless. This was the thing, apparently, that kept driving a wedge between Min and me. And I couldn't see a way out of it. Everything I did to counter who I was—no stable job, the tattoos, the spoken-word gigs, the pick-up games—only seemed to persuade other white guys that I was one of theirs. In Italy it was immediately clear when the person I was talking to reached to shake my hand; he'd go for my forearm in that weird Il Duce thing they all do.

It had all started to worry me. After all, didn't I keep on reading, and trying to understand, Ezra Pound? Hadn't I repeatedly walked to the little house of Pound's partner, Olga Rudge, there in Venice on the Calle Querini—always at dusk? Her name was still on the door and on a handwritten slip of paper above the bell. She'd been dead for more than twenty years, but someone clearly lived there. Every time I walked down the silent, echoing street and stopped in front of the building, I saw curtains flutter at the top window and heard the bang of closing shutters.

I didn't even like reading Pound, really. I'd claimed to understand him in college, but that was mostly an act. I had a kind of connection to him—not really, but kind of. My mother's "patron" after my father left us, an old woman who was one of the last heirs to a giant pharmaceutical fortune, left a big chunk of that fortune to a magazine Pound had written for in the 1920s. She'd left an even bigger chunk to my mom, and a bigger one than that to my father, who was her grand-nephew.

Now here was Stefan, noticing my copy of *The Cantos*, and my tattoo. My blithe "Americanness," in his words, my confidence in speaking to him but also my stupidity in paying money, on numerous occasions, to hear him and his fellow musicians play over-cooked Vivaldi. Basically in their sleep. There I'd sat, more than once, among the other tourist sheep. He'd spotted me right away, Stefan said.

He'd been apolitical for most of his life, he told me that first night as we drank grappa in a bar tucked behind the Campo Manin. But recently he'd joined up with CasaPound. Well, one didn't necessarily "join," he said; he went to rallies, he listened to some of their speakers. He did in fact have political views, he realized; it was just that before CasaPound, he hadn't found a political party or group that spoke to them. Suspicion of global capital, and banks. Housing for poor working Europeans. Clear, and definite, borders. Work, and fair housing, for Italians. For the Germans and the Czechs, the French, the English. But not for the Africans or the Arabs who had left their home countries.

Surely I shared similar feelings, he said, as an American.

"Not exactly," I said, but mostly I kept quiet. I'd been messing with right-wing assholes for years by then—listening to them, pretending to take them seriously, even sometimes paying the tab. Then dodging the stupid handshake and maybe spitting on them, or worse. Telling them to fuck themselves or go to hell or whatever brilliant riposte came to my drunken mind.

By the way, I sometimes explained while I signed the credit card slip, the owl tattoo was for my girlfriend. Who was Dominican. Whose mother named her Minerva, because she liked Roman mythology.

"You probably wouldn't expect that of a poor woman from the islands who barely spoke English when she arrived here, right?" I'd say. "That woman probably learned more in her six years in a rural school in the D.R. than you did in four years in your bullshit suburban American high school. You stupid fuck."

Often I was too wasted to know whether I actually said such things out loud or not. It hardly ever mattered. Usually I was bigger, and stronger, than whatever white guy in a polo shirt I was fucking with. Sometimes, when I wasn't, I got a little roughed up. But if there was a fight, I usually came out on top.

I was bigger and stronger than Stefan, no question. But he wasn't wearing a polo shirt and khakis, or expensive jeans and an untucked button-down. He was wearing cheap black pants and a black collared shirt, the chamber group's uniform. He had no visible tattoos, his beard needed a trim, and his wire-rimmed glasses were greasy and smudged. He looked more like one of my college professors than like the other neofascists I'd met. And when I told him about my tattoo, and Min, what he said—after asking for the tenth cigarette of the night—was, "This is very interesting to me. I would like for you to explain more about what it is to be 'Dominican,' and about your view of North American borders."

None of the skinheads I'd met in pubs in London, and none of the red-faced white guys I met playing pool in bars back home, had ever asked me to explain my own position, much less how this "position" matched up with my interest in the fascist-sympathizing poet Ezra Pound. So instead of calling for the check and telling Stefan to go fuck himself, I ordered more grappa.

• • •

I HAD A MISERABLE HANGOVER the next day, and I was nearly an hour late for my shift at Prima dell'alluvione. Tomasso was visibly annoyed, which annoyed *me*; it wasn't like he was paying me.

When I told him where I'd been the night before, about the concert and meeting Stefan, he shook his head.

"You shouldn't trust someone from CasaPound," he said.

I didn't necessarily *trust* this guy, I told him. But on the other hand, I'd never before met a right-wing white guy who, once he realized we had basically nothing in common, was still willing to listen to anything I had to say.

"Oh, they will gladly listen to you," Tomasso said as he pulled his jacket from the hook by the door. "They will listen to you as long as you'd like."

He opened the door to a gust of wind and a splash of rain. The floods from the week before had barely receded, and it was pouring again. "They will listen to you, and then they will calmly explain to you why you are wrong. Nationalists can see no other future. And they are very persuasive. Soon he will begin to talk to you about all you have to lose." He opened his umbrella and stepped out the door, somehow managing to shrug, in his very Venetian way, as he did so. "And of course he will not be wrong," he added, smiling. Then he closed the door and headed home for his lunch and nap.

Here was another way in which Tomasso's advice did not seem helpful. I'd heard him rail against CasaPound and other right-wing factions before; I knew where he stood on these matters. Pound's books might have been prominently displayed in coffee shops and bars in working-class neighborhoods all over Italy, especially in Rome. I knew they were— I'd seen them, and I'd found it strange until I learned about CasaPound. But Tomasso refused to stock Pound's work. No fan of Mussolini was welcome in Prima dell'alluvione, he said. Also, national borders were nothing but a quaint relic of the past. Tomasso favored open borders; he spent his days on the internet and found borders of any kind ludicrous, he said, "at this point in human history."

He reminded me of other people I knew. People who claimed to want revolution, systemic change and all that. But who didn't necessarily want to be in the middle of any of it. Tomasso, like many of the people I met in Venice—bartenders, clerks in stores selling glass and leather and commedia dell'arte masks—was counting the days until he had enough money to get out. He wanted to leave Venice, wanted to move someplace in the north or maybe even the south, someplace quieter, more rural. Without so many tourists, without so much stress and worry over money.

And without all this business with migrants, those people sometimes said. Or when it wasn't said, it was implied.

Tomasso even had the typical northern Italian's snobbery about the south. "Not Napoli," he told me, wanting to be clear. "And not Palermo. The countryside." When he said that, he sounded like another of my mother's boyfriends, a man from Rome who was an executive at an international cement company. Most Italian restaurants in the U.S., that guy told me, were for shit. "They're all owned by Sicilians."

A week or so after that conversation with Tomasso I had plans to meet Stefan in Dorsoduro, where he was staying at a friend's place until the concert series at the church would end in a few weeks; after that he would head to Rome to perform with a chamber orchestra there through the fall. I was early, so I decided to stop by Olga Rudge's house and stare at the door one more time.

It was Olga Rudge who cared for old Ezra in the years before he died in 1972. After he was accused of treason at the end of the Second World War and spent thirteen years, from 1945 to 1958, in a psychiatric hospital in Washington, DC. "The bughouse" he called it—but it could have been worse; he could have been executed for his pro-Mussolini radio broadcasts during the war.

Olga Rudge loved him anyway, and why? Because of his poetry? His intellect? His wife's money? That part I could never figure out. I also had a ridiculous fantasy about meeting up with his daughter, who was in her nineties by the time I got to Venice but apparently sometimes stayed in the little house on the Calle Querini. She was Ezra and Olga's "child out of wedlock," as people called it back then. A bastard child. Like me.

I thought, at one time, that this was one thing that might keep Min and me together: the fact that both of us barely knew our fathers. Mine sent me Christmas cards once a year and, in recent years, invitations to gallery openings of his truly bad paintings. I know basically nothing about art, but even I can tell they're bad. He's been painting for maybe five years at this point, but that doesn't prevent him from getting shows in places like Santa Fe and Key West. That's another thing money can get you: undeserved recognition for pretty much anything you do.

Min never met her dad; in a reversal of the usual journey, her mom was sent to the U.S. when she became pregnant at nineteen. She moved into a tiny apartment in the building where her two younger brothers and their families lived.

Her mom was the family oddball, Min said. According to Min's cousins, the rumor was that her father was a Haitian field worker. Hadn't Min wondered, this cousin asked, why she was so dark?

I loved Min's family, and they seemed to like me. I played ball or video games with her older cousins, let her little cousins ride around on my back and shoulders, drank beer and watched soccer with her uncles. The only person who seemed uncertain about me was Min's mom. I could tell she didn't really trust me. I told myself it was because Min's father had abandoned them, but deep down I knew that wasn't it. She thought I was toying with Min. She thought I was a rich white boy who was just slumming when I came to Reading to be with her daughter. I heard her say it, more than once. She didn't know how much Spanish I actually understood.

The thing is, maybe I *was* slumming. I loved Min, but would I have moved to Reading to live with her? Maybe not; I didn't really know. But I didn't need to move to Reading to be with her; she was in Philadelphia now, sharing an apartment with two other girls from college, all of them nurses at different hospitals.

Min wouldn't live with me, in Philadelphia or anywhere else. Not till I had a job, she said, even though I didn't need one. She had some principles about that. She'd let me spend nights in her apartment, in her bed, for a while. During the year when we were first out of school, before she moved into her apartment and when she was still driving back and forth to Reading after her shifts at the hospital, sometimes she spent the night with me at my mom's house. But only when my mom was away. I understood that. My mom—who can be too intense and tends to drink too much and seems clueless about things like her own economic advantages—has scared away a lot of my friends through the years.

I loved Min. And I loved Reading, though Min never believed me when I said that. I liked the old brick rowhouses— one of them marked with a plaque because Wallace Stevens was born there, but I didn't mention it to Min when I drove over to look at it on my own. I also liked all the signs in Spanish in the center of the city, the crowded blocks below the steep hill people called Mount Penn.

There was a weird Chinese pagoda at the top of that hill. It was built early in the twentieth century and was supposed to be part of a resort that never actually got built. Reading was all about past glory and past wealth—railroads, industry, all of that gone now. I loved that because I was pretty certain it was how most of the United States was going to look eventually—like a big, abandoned strip mall. That should have made me sad, Min told me. The fact that it just made me laugh was another reason she didn't really think we belonged together.

Min and I had sex for the first time in the parking lot outside that pagoda, on a frigid January day during our sophomore year. It was Christmas break, and I was driving up to

Reading every chance I got, taking every opportunity over that holiday to avoid my own house in Lower Merion.

"I used to come here all the time," Min said as we sat in my car, the engine running and the heater roaring. We took turns taking sips from a bottle of expensive whiskey that I'd brought along. "To warm up," we said, but we both knew it was to help us relax and do what we'd come there to do.

My long legs were folded and cramped there on the back seat of my Jeep Cherokee, but I didn't mind. I was feeling no pain, and not because of the whiskey. Because of Min, because of how heavenly she smelled, and the quiet little moans she made, and the rush to my brain when she took me in her hand, and then her mouth.

How do you begin to explain something like a Chinese pagoda in a decaying post-industrial city like Reading, Pennsylvania, to someone like Stefan, a neofascist violinist from the Czech Republic? Or what it means to fall as hard as I fell for someone like Min, someone so beautiful, and competent, and gentle—a dedicated student and even more dedicated nurse, whose job, and life, remain precarious in a place like the United States. Where nurses like Min are needed, but where nurses like Min aren't entirely legal.

I couldn't believe that someone as smart and thoughtful as Stefan would think that national borders should come first, always. Ahead of competence. Ahead of love. If she married me, that would solve everything, Stefan pointed out one night at a cafe on the vast Piazzo San Marco where once again I was buying the drinks. But that infuriated Min, as I tried to explain to him. That marrying someone like me could make her suddenly acceptable as a citizen, while her skills as a nurse and her faithful payment of taxes could not.

At first Stefan had been curious about my love for Min, about this young woman from the Dominican Republic with a name that had ancient European roots. I thought he'd been curious for generous and intelligent reasons. I'd thought, I suppose, that he was an intelligent and gifted man who dallied with things like racism and xenophobic nationalism but could also respond to reason. Like Wallace Stevens as a matter of fact. Like Ezra Pound (though he did more than dally with those things). Surely Stefan could be convinced by the very reasonable proposition that Min's refusal to marry me in order to get a green card was evidence of her suitability for full American citizenship. She wasn't looking for an easy way to do it. She wouldn't complicate love in that way.

But, "All this proves is that you are a fool," he said to me that night. And he repeated this observation on his last night in Venice, when I invited him to join me at one of the art collective openings in the palazzo where I was staying.

. . .

WE'D BEEN ARGUING about the new work that was on display in the ground-level gallery. These were works by three women, all created as tributes to an earlier painter, a kind of outsider Italian artist named Carol Rama. Painted faces with scrotums for ears. Wax effigies of genitals. And my personal favorite, because it spoke to me particularly, brightly colored neon coils in the shape of a penis and balls, perched inside a basketball hoop.

"This is such horrible shit," Stefan said, crossing the room and polishing off the third drink I'd bought him that night before grabbing my arm to pull me toward the door. "It is nihilistic propaganda, not art."

For some reason this enraged me. I thought of my father's lame landscapes—adobe churches from the American Southwest rendered with no understanding of perspective, waves splashing on rocks somewhere in northern California, a pink-orange sunset seen, of course, from the pier in Key West. Then I thought of Stefan and his fellow musicians and their nightly sleepwalking through soulless performances of *The Four Seasons*.

"Who the fuck are you to pass judgment on this?" I snarled at him, yanking my arm free. I thought I was only snarling, but I'd just polished off my own fourth drink, and it was loud in the gallery. Apparently I was actually shouting. Our argument built from there, and before long Teresa, who managed the gallery and handled the renting of rooms, was at my side, asking if we would please take our discussion outside.

Which we did. And which is how I suddenly found myself perched at the edge of the *rio terra*, teetering above the Rio di San Luca canal.

"All Americans like you are the same," Stefan yelled at me. "Italians like you also. Dreamers, fantasists, all of you—you ignore the natural order. Borders exist for a reason. In most cases these are natural barriers. From what you have told me I believe this woman you love, this *Mee-naer-va*, this hot island girl with a Roman goddess's name, she understands all of this far better than you ever will. All your money, all the wealth you did not earn yourself—it has made you feel enormous guilt. And that guilt has made you blind."

Maybe, probably, the thing that pissed me off the most was that what Stefan was saying that night sounded like things Min had said to me too. Often, in fact, in recent years. She could take care of herself; she *was* taking care of herself. She was more productive and self-sufficient than I would ever be. My nation's government, and its tax structure, had long ago ensured that I would never have to earn my own way as she and her mother had done all their lives. And if the government decided that, in fact, after all that—after working multiple shit jobs and paying for her own education and taking a job as a nurse in a hospital where other nurses, white ones, did not want to work—she still did not deserve a shot at citizenship, a chance to stay, then she was not going to attach herself, through marriage, to a white man to get them to look the other way.

That might have been the real root of my rage. But it's not what I focused on that night. I was fixated on the fact that Stefan had called Min a hot island girl. That he'd said her name with an exaggerated accent that dripped with contempt.

I reached to grab him by his upper arms. I was on the verge of head-butting him. He went limp as I grabbed him, and I saw genuine fear in his eyes.

But I hadn't realized how close I was to the edge. When I pushed him away instead, I took an unsteady step back. But there was nothing there, and I was falling, all six and half feet of me awkwardly falling, into the cold, black water, into the wake of a gondola that had passed just seconds before.

I laughed as I fell, amazed that it had happened this way. I let myself sink, somehow curious about the water's depth but not thinking of anything really, just the silliness of how it all came to pass. But then, out of nowhere, I flashed on a scene from several nights before. That night had been clear, and a bit warmer, and the bars and cafes had their outdoor tables set up again. I was at a table by myself, smoking cigarettes and drinking beer and trying, yet again, to read the

Cantos. I looked up to see two uniformed ambulance boat operators rolling an old man, strapped tightly in a wheelchair, to the pier at the end of the narrow street.

Imagine being rolled in front of all these people drinking neon-orange spritzes, I thought that night, averting my eyes as they rolled the old guy past me. There in your pajamas with your bare feet sticking out while everyone watches you getting wheeled to the water's edge. Imagine being alone in a city like Venice, when you're as old as that old man.

Imagine if Olga Rudge hadn't been there, willing to wait while Ezra was accused of treason, then held in a cage on a military base near Pisa for three weeks before he landed in a mental hospital in the U.S. Imagine her, when he was finally released and his wife and official guardian was no longer willing to care for him, taking him into her home. Imagine if Pound hadn't had her.

My head broke the surface of the Rio di San Luca a good twenty feet downstream from where I'd fallen in. Slowly and deliberately, still thinking about wasted old Ezra, I gripped the slimy edge of the canal and pulled myself sideways, back toward the end of the *rio terra*. As I neared the palazzo Stefan came and reached down to help me up just as another gondola floated languidly by, its gondolier playing an amplified accordion loud enough to wake the dead. Other people were stumbling out of the gallery by then, pulling out their phones and taking photos and videos. Of me.

I coughed a couple times and then said "Thanks."

But I didn't really feel grateful to Stefan. I wished I had pulled him in with me. Better yet, I wished I had caught my balance and swung around and thrown him in instead, then walked away and left him there.

I started walking, taking note of nothing around me. I barely saw the laughing people outside the gallery watching me or the gawking tourists I passed as I approached the Fenice opera house. I was focused, instead, on certain pictures that kept floating through my mind. Once again I saw that old man in the wheelchair, in his gray and threadbare pajamas. Craggy old Ezra with his beard and his crazy eyes and the wild pile of hair on top of his head. Wallace Stevens's bulldog face and his somber insurance salesman's suit. Old white guys at the end of their lives, nothing left to do but let them strap you in and take you to some hospital someplace else. That's all I could think about as I walked and walked that night, soaked to the bone and shivering in the autumn air.

Until hours later, when I came back to my room and stripped off my wet clothes, crawled into bed, and focused on the memory of Min's face. Until I finally fell asleep, determined to call her, one more time, the next day.

The Dime Museum

CHICAGO, 1965

TOM, MAUDE'S MAKE-BELIEVE GRANDSON, has called to tell her he's enlisted. (Something she already knows.) He'll join the Army before they can draft him, he says. See a bit of the world, maybe come out with more on the other side. If he comes out the other side. And both of them laugh. Maude says she wouldn't know which would be better— his coming out the other side or his not coming out the other side. She's thinking, though, why not the shortest run you could make of it? Or why not a straight path up through Michigan, across the border to the other side? That's what she would have expected of poor, bedeviled young Tom, their little Tommy, nineteen years old and living God knows where, maybe on the streets, and smoking so much he coughs like a man three times his age.

He wants to come see her, he says, to hear some of the old stories. I want you to tell me more, Non, he's said to her. Non short for Nonny, what he called her from the time he could talk. She told him some stories in the past, mostly that time they traveled together by train, from Chicago to Philadelphia. She's told him some stories and she could tell him more, many more, but she isn't sure he'd want to hear them. Like how they came to spend that summer week, when he was a boy, with a rich and drunken madwoman (or so Annie's children and stepchildren had seen her, as a drunk and a madwoman who needed tethering). How she, Maude, and young Tom had been summarily dismissed from the fancy old hotel in Cape May. It hadn't just been time to start the next part of that trip. Despite what she'd told him.

Well, she might tell him another tale or two now. Sing some of the old songs with him. "Knees Up Mother Brown," "Burlington Bertie," "When the Right Girl Comes Along" and—this would be a good one now—"Oh! It's a Lovely War." She'd liked that one especially, how you could sing one thing and mean another. That was the first massive war of her lifetime, a ridiculous one but maybe not as ridiculous as this new one in Asia. Who can say? The men in charge claim to know what they're doing, but then that's always been the case. Over and over, they're proved wrong but who even notices? The poets maybe. But who listens to them anymore?

Young Tom will want to hear his favorite tune from the time he was a baby. *After the ball is over,* Maude remembers crooning to him. *After the break of morn.* She sang better when she used to rock him to sleep than she'd ever done on a stage. She remembers her old rooms on North Clark Street, late morning light pouring through the filmy curtains, rousing dust from the clutter. The tea set she'd once shared with Annie—a gift to them, from the owner of the Gem, at their so-called wedding fifty years ago. Her threadbare blankets and quilts. Her books in neat stacks on a shelf below the window. Outside, people honking their auto horns and shouting.

From her chair, rocking the weepy boy on her knee, she could see the Checker cabs backed up below her second-floor window, waiting to make the turn onto the avenue. Her window would have been open, even in the dead of winter. Year-round there was a cold wind from the lake. It ruffled the curtains and gave the room a chill. She might have closed the window, shut out the cold and the automobile exhaust, but she had read that the cool air was good for a baby's sleep.

Everything she knew she'd read somewhere—in a book from the library, or a newspaper or magazine. Maybe, she sometimes thinks, this was her problem. But it was a kind of miracle too, wasn't it? How she'd come to know what she knew. To work where she'd worked. To have helped raise this boy—now a man, now ready to do what they all seemed bent on doing, to be a soldier, go to war. No talking him out of it, Prue has said. His other make-believe granny. Prue short for Prudence, her full given name, which she hated. Though it suited her, Maude had told her many times, because she was always the prudent one. And it's a good thing one of us was, Prue liked to say, though it wasn't exactly prudence that had gotten the two of them—first Maude, then Prue—the job that had kept their little makeshift family afloat.

They'd been secretaries at a library. A favorite of Chicago's cultural elite from the time of its founding in 1887, handily growing and in need of more staff when Maude finished her secretarial classes in 1922.

Mr. Josephs, the collections director, had been Maude's boss and now he was Prue's. Though she'll retire soon also. But she won't live here, in this little piece of bedlam by the lake where Maude now gets to live. There's a carriage house waiting for Prue behind her sister's house in Irving Park, all furnished and ready for her. Maude is also welcome there, Prue has told her, though Maude sincerely doubts it. She won't be going there, and neither will Tom. He's refused to set foot in that house, even on that block, since the day he turned eighteen and learned the truth.

Mr. Josephs also loved her stories. That's how she'd learned to parcel them out, bit by bit. The first one—a true one, only changed a little—had gotten her the job as his secretary forty years ago. That was the one about the night she'd spent in the rooms of the famous poet.

Speaking of it to Mr. Josephs she'd called herself a member of a touring theatre troupe. She'd been careful not to say vaudeville. He was so young then, barely out of college at the University of Chicago, blond and eager in his tie and cufflinks and ill-fitting suit. An elfin, breathless literature student whose father had made a suitable donation to the library and so ensured his job.

Was it Shakespeare they'd done, he'd asked her? And she'd murmured something, "A bit, yes . . ." and tried to change the subject. Another time, when he asked, she'd veered a little closer to the truth. "A little of everything, as best I can recall. Even a bit of song and dance." It was all so long ago, she'd said, then closed her steno pad and briskly left his office.

Should she tell Tom the stories she's never told anyone else? The truths she hid from Mr. Josephs, even from Prue? Some of the earliest ones she remembers. About what a failure she'd been at that other thing, that other life as a performer. Or about her time as a dime museum caricature. How could she explain it, the fact the happiest time of her life was that period, starting sometime during the Great War, when people had paid to gawk at her as she sat on a stool, wearing trousers and suspenders and a monocle over her eye?

At her and Annie. At her and the only person she's ever loved. Besides little Tom. And well yes, her mother and father. For a time.

Sing for your papa, little Maudie, her father used to say. He'd be drunk, then snoring, then remorseful and glum.

Mourning her mother, mourning their lives back in London, before they'd decided to take their little girl and try their luck in the U.S. In Chicago of all places—a city known to the world, suddenly, because of the World's Columbian Exposition—where they'd followed a shiftless promoter who cornered them backstage at the Alhambra in London one night. The work he'd promised them at a new theatre on Halstead Street in Chicago had been nothing but a puff of smoke from his carved ivory pipe—a flat-out lie. Same as the so-called theatre; when they showed up at the address atop the meaningless "investment agreement" he'd persuaded them to sign, and pay for, they'd found a butcher shop.

And so they'd gone on the road—*The Singing Davies Family, fresh from the London Stage!*—until her mother died of tuberculosis when Maude was twelve, in the winter of 1900. After that came a few years with the hoboes on West Madison and before long she was dressing as a little man and singing for tips, faking a high-pitched Irish brogue. Soon she was back on the road, this time on her own. Her father was in Rosehill Cemetery.

Such a tiny little thing, bones like a little bird, voice like a mockin'bird's. Her father's view of her as a child had been all wrong, or mostly wrong, the product of bathtub gin and maudlin sentiment. She'd been thin, but also strong. And she sang, but not that well. For a while she'd believed him. It's probably what led her to the fond and foolish notion that she might someday be a poet. That, and the books of her mother's she'd carried with her since her death—Shakespeare's Sonnets, Byron's *Childe Harold's Pilgrimage*, Kipling's *Barrack Room Ballads*. They'd traveled with Maude from flophouse to riverside camp to the rooms on North Clark, where they sat on their makeshift shelf in the place where she stayed for forty years, watching the neighborhood surge and shift all around her, tossed by a storm of postwar money.

Now that building and others like it are gone. No more rooms for single lodgers like Maude, except maybe here in "the home," as Prue calls it—to which Maude replies, you mean the poorhouse. The Bughouse Square hoboes are long gone and now the square's a pretty park where employees of the library sit on benches and open their lunch bags on sunny days in summer. The Anarchist Book Shop—in its tiny store-front two doors away from the entrance to her old building on Clark Street—is long closed. Some of the fellows who'd congregated in the park or in the book shop ended up in jail or in Russia, who knew where they all went.

Except for Maude's neighbor, Tom Senior, the book shop owner, Prue's father and little Tommy's great-grandfather. By the early twenties Tom Senior was back in the neighborhood after his years in prison downstate, his spirit broken. Twenty-five years after that he was long dead, and his granddaughter had shamed the family with her unwanted pregnancy. And Maude had agreed with Prue that they would raise the girl's son, Prue's nephew, as their grandson before they'd let Prue's sister Rose—more married to the Catholic church than to the shiftless Irish brute, in Prue's words, who was her husband—turn him over to the real nuns.

Maude *had* met the famous poet, back in 1908. This much was true. But how she had come to drop this into the conversation at her interview for the job at the library, she can't recall. She knows only that Mr. Josephs never forgot it, and that it must have been why he'd hired her. Years later, after she'd retired and Prue had taken over her job, he started sending articles home with Prue for Maude to read. About the poet's arrest, the charges of treason, and more. Some of these she'd already seen in the newspaper; she'd been mildly interested, mostly confused. Mostly she hadn't especially wanted to remember the nights she'd spent with him forty years before.

And then there was the article about the prize the poet's friends insisted he should receive, traitor or not. He was awarded $1,000; she remembers being stunned by the amount and wondering, what was he to do with that kind of money in a mental asylum? Though of course he didn't stay there.

She didn't know all of what he'd said on the radio during the war, in Italy. She'd wondered about it idly but had never been able to learn much, at least at first. Though she thought she could probably imagine the kinds of things he would say, from knowing him so briefly years before. She thought he'd place himself in the center of it all—the center of a war even—with a bluster that could steal the breath of everyone else in the room. It's what he'd done with all of them in that cold little town somewhere to the south, in Indiana, she's forgotten the name. There was a college there, where he taught. And she and others from the troupe had played cards and drunk whiskey and cheap rum in his boardinghouse rooms, the first time she was there with the traveling show.

The second time was just a few months later, and it was one of the times she didn't care to remember, when her voice had failed and angry men in the smoke-filled audience had harangued her off the stage. Others in the company—all of them, even generous old Molly the costume manager—lost patience with her that night and left her wandering around the streets of the town at midnight. In a snowstorm. As drunk as her father had ever been.

The poet had found her by the station in the biting cold of that upright village surrounded by farms. He'd walked out at midnight to post a letter. He'd moved by then, to nicer rooms in a house owned by two stern old biddies. Maude could still laugh at that part at least, remembering the looks on their faces in the morning.

He was confident to the point of arrogance. But she'd liked him. He'd been good to her. What might have happened to her, that bitter night in the snow, if he hadn't found her? If he hadn't said to leave that miserable troupe, to find another way to live?

And what has happened to that china tea pot? The one she'd shared with Annie, their wedding gift from the owner of the Gem, the place where she'd next found work. Where she and Annie had performed for the customers, for the clink and clatter of all their silver dimes. *And for the grand finale, the marriage of Mick and Minerva!* Then came the titters from the blushing women, the cigar-choked belly laughs from the men.

They hadn't known, any of them, how deeply Maude had meant it when she said, *I take you. I will love and cherish you.* She'd worn her old tux and tails from her vaudeville days, the monocle that kept slipping from the socket of her eye.

When she knew him, briefly, almost sixty years ago, the poet was teaching French and Greek to the boys at the college. Things she'd longed to learn, to know. And writing poems of his own. Something she'd also foolishly dreamed of doing back then.

• • •

"AFTER THE BALL" may have been Tommy's favorite as a boy but now he listens to rock and roll and smokes more cigarettes in a day than Maude ever did, even at her worst.

The emphysema will likely kill her, but the war might kill him first. Or so she plans to tell him. Better that than the stories he thinks he wants to hear. No one really wants to hear them, not when she gets to the bare root of it all. Which is the love she felt only once in her life and lost not once but twice.

When her touring life was finished, she'd felt tremendous relief. But there was rent to pay for her boardinghouse room, and so she'd found work at the Gem. There, for a time, she was The Bogus Man. There were other male impersonators in those days, famous ones, and what people loved about them was the magic. The way those women transformed themselves, the womanly curves and bounteous breasts they'd hidden below trousers and suspenders—then showed off in gowns and pearls after the show. But in a dime museum no one cared how Maude looked after the show, after she sat on her stool—not moving, hardly blinking—and looked for all the world like a man. Which was the same as she looked after the show.

At the dime shows they'd have sooner spat on you than applaud your womanly magic. So she could be skinny, chicken-legged Irish Mick in the clothing she preferred, a stiff-collared shirt and cravat and suspendered trousers, her hair cut short and blackened with dye. She was The Bogus Man, sandwiched between emaciated Karl—The Living Skeleton—and The Missing Link, a black man named Ezekiel with a burlap bag wrapped around his privates and a bone that he somehow hooked inside his nose. Soon after Maude started, Annie showed up to be The Fat Lady.

When she married Annie, Ezekiel sang a hymn that began "There is a balm in Gilead," and Maude had held on to that word, *balm*, not because of anything to do with Jesus but because of what it meant to her, which was what Annie had offered her. She felt that Ezekiel had understood this somehow. To Maude, Annie was a balm, a comfort. Big soft waves of balm when Annie wrapped Maude in her pillowy arms and thighs and rocked her against her sweet soft belly and her giant breasts.

Balm was what a body could become when it was more than just a thing for leering at, or for mocking. Though Annie *was* a beauty to behold. Her skin was china-doll smooth, her lush, dark brown hair perfectly crimped and curled. She had the kind of mouth they called a rosebud, and her breath was always clean and sweet, smelling of apricots and berries when they kissed. Maude should have known that a beauty like that, whatever its size, could not be hers to keep.

When Annie arrived at the Gem they set her up next to Maude The Bogus Man. They played their roles (*The man who's really a woman! The fattest woman in the city of Chicago!*) in silence, sitting on their respective stools for hours and then collecting their portion of the till at the end of the night. On the weekends sometimes they performed as The Marvelous Mick and Minerva, singing a couple of the old songs, dancing a little—an act in which they essentially played themselves. She was Mick, mincing around the stage and mooning over his imposing beloved; Annie was the giant, beloved Minerva at the center of the stage, capable of squashing Mick and lasciviously threatening to do so. They sang in comical harmony, Maude in her never quite on-key alto, Annie's voice even deeper, a convincing baritone.

For nearly ten years Annie was Maude's unspeakable, passionate love. The one she'd been longing for, though she hadn't revealed this—not to anyone else or even, really, to herself—back when she was part of the traveling troupe. Back when she wrote yearning, lovesick poems on scraps of paper and carried them with her in the pockets of her frayed gentleman's trousers. Mostly secret, lovesick odes to other girls in the show.

Maude hadn't loved the idea of caring for Tommy at first. Yes, she'd sometimes looked after Prue and Rose when they were girls, when their parents were out late at meetings downtown, and later when Tom Senior disappeared somewhere on a bender. But she'd never cared for an infant in her life, and neither had Prue. But there were books, Prue reminded her—their answer to everything. Years of working amongst bookish people could make you think yourself capable of learning about practically anything, once you'd read the right book.

Even poetry. Even the famous poet's strange, basically unreadable later work. (Maude had tried, with the book that won the prize.) After that first article about the prize, Mr. Josephs kept sending more. These were from the *Partisan Review* and the *Saturday Review of Literature*. "Be warned," he'd instructed Prue to tell Maude, "the first is legitimate, the second strictly a middlebrow affair."

The poet seemed to have one chief preoccupation during the war, and that was money. But wasn't that everyone's? He'd managed to make even these things, money and the banks and the gold standard, into an intellectual endeavor that he had also mastered, along with history and languages and the entire continent of Asia. When she'd known him—not really known him, only drunk rum with him and played cards in one of his abodes and then slept for a night in another—he'd spoken a strange soup of French and flat middle American jingoisms.

On the first night in his rooms years ago, amidst the card playing and drinking, the smoking and singing and reciting, a few of the more daring college boys had looked up from where they sat at the poet's feet to stare at Wanda, the willowy dancer who'd flirted brazenly with the poet but all the while kept one eye on the older college boy she'd leave with. All of it made Maude jealous, the way the poet and his students spoke in unknown languages and recited lines from poems, some of which she'd recognized (a line or two of Kipling, a little bit of Whitman) though she hadn't dared join in. She remembers all of that now and still feels a twinge of shame at the memory.

Of course they'd all seen it, all of them from the show— how much she'd wanted what those college boys had. The language, the poetry, the unabashed desire for beautiful Wanda. And the poet, with his soft shirt and flowing tie and colorful socks and broad-brimmed hat on a hook by the door, had seen it too. Maude dreamed of having Wanda look at her the way she looked at the poet and at the college boys, all blinking eyes and flushed cheeks and breathy laughter, all smoldering sex there below her kitten-purr coyness. That may have been why, when they were back to do that disastrous second show, they'd let Maude drift out on her own from the town's only bar, why they'd let her go and not come after her. Maybe they were disgusted with her, and not just because of her dreadful singing.

She was looking for the poet's old boardinghouse that second night in the town, but small as the town was, in the heavy snow and in her drunken state she couldn't find it. All of them were drunk and disconsolate that night. They'd barely sold enough tickets to pay their way back, and they'd given up when half of the handful of ticket buyers had booed and hissed and walked out before the first intermission.

It was all right for Maude to be who she was when the show was well received, when they were making money. But when the show failed, somehow it always seemed to be her fault. The rest of them had made the last train out of town that night while she was still out there, wandering the streets.

The poet was a strangely handsome man, and brilliant. She could recognize his brilliance then, and she'd seen it again in the book that won the prize, despite its thick, impenetrable slurry of words that made her eyes hurt as she tried to read. He was brilliant and arrogant, but he'd been kind to her.

"You can stay in my rooms and take the morning train," he'd said.

"It's all right. I'll sleep at my office."

And, "You shouldn't try to be the kind of person they insist on. You should be whoever you believe that you are."

The middlebrow writers in the *Saturday Review of Literature* said some very damning things about him. He'd called President Roosevelt Franklin Delano Jewsfeld and Finkelstein and Roosenstein on the radio in Italy. He'd said the banks were run by Jews and usurers and that democracy was a joke.

With men, all conflict seems, in the end, to be about money. This is what she plans to tell young Tom. You don't need to hear my stories, she plans to say. Just listen to my advice. If you go, you'll be fighting a rich man's war. That's the way it always goes.

Money, for Maude, has always been nothing but a nagging inconvenience, and of course now it's the reason she'll live out the rest of her days in this house of wracked bodies and fearful delusions and frequent screaming. At least she has her own room, her books, and a few other belongings tucked in boxes under the bed, and from the corner of her window, a view of blue Lake Michigan. She hadn't understood the things the poet said about social credit theory; she hadn't even felt like trying to understand. When she thinks of gold and silver, what she recalls is the beautiful new Mercury dime in 1916, with its lovely head of Lady Liberty. A heavy handful in her pocket, sifting through her fingers as she leaned her head on Annie's shoulder on the long rides home. The happiest days of her life were those days of the dime shows at the Gem, of sitting on a stool as The Bogus Man and ignoring all the leering and the insults and looking only at The Fat Lady. At Annie. Catching her eye and smiling, her heart leaping when Annie smiled back, winking at her.

Back then, they'd held on until they could take their cut and then ridden the new elevated train to the peace of their shared rooms. No one minded as they passed among the hoboes camped around Bughouse Square, the air smelling of the smoke of the hoboes' fires, the bits of cheap meat they were roasting. No one looked twice at fat Annie or at little Maude, the child performer some of them remembered, now with her hair cut short and always dressed as a man.

Once home in their rooms, the same North Side rooms where Maude lived for years, they could reach for each other at last. And Maude could fall asleep in the welcoming folds of Annie's warm body, her yeasty flesh as rich as cake.

They were together for a pleasant blur of years, until the new decade, the 1920s, and the arrival of Mr. Milford, a sixty-year-old widower who paid his shiny new dime (and who could have paid a great deal more) and recognized The Fat Lady's beauty and brought her a copy of a different sort of book, Lulu Hunt Peters's *Diet and Health*. Soon after Annie came home with a suit of rubber to wear under her clothes, and before long she'd lost a good number of the rolls in her flesh. She became more beautiful than ever, now only pleasantly plump. And she became engaged to Mr. Milford, who had once made pills in his North Side apartment and now owned successful alkaloidal laboratories in Chicago and Philadelphia.

Before she left, Annie persuaded her wealthy husband to write a check for her poor friend Maude. Her roommate, she'd called her. He'd winked and said he'd never found little Mick a very convincing man and pulled a fountain pen from his pocket with a great flourish, there in the theatre lobby.

"Use it for a course at business school," Annie said, and so Maude had. She'd failed as a traveling vaudevillian, as a woman who mysteriously transformed into a man onstage. After that she'd sat on a stool as The Bogus Man, then clowned onstage with her partner and her one great love, The Fat Lady. That had been tolerable only as long as Annie remained on the stool next to hers and sang the silly old songs alongside her.

So she became a secretary.

* * *

FAMILY IS EVERYTHING. This is what Rose, Prue's sister and the matriarch of the house in Irving Park, said in 1956. That was the year Tommy was invited, forced really, to move in with his true grandparents—Rose and her brute—and his mother, who had returned, ten years after his birth, a bit worse for wear. She was introduced to Tommy as his older sister.

He never really settled into that contorted family. He grew into a sullen and angry teenager, same as his mother/sister had been, according to Prue. He'd prowled the streets with other angry, motherless boys, getting into fights. Some nights he'd slept on the floor in Maude's room, though she'd tried to discourage this. Not to worry, he told her. He'd say he stayed over at a friend's. Which wasn't really lying. Not that he minded lying to his grandmother, he said. Not in the least.

Rose had decreed that he would learn the truth about his mother/sister when he turned eighteen and finished high school. When they told him, Prue reported on the telephone a year ago, he'd said "Fuck you all." He'd said he wanted nothing to do with any of them. He'd said he was going to move in with Maude. With Non.

Though of course he couldn't move in with her in the old folks' home. Not in the poorhouse. Prue tried to persuade him to move into her tidy little apartment near the library. He could sleep on her sofa, she said. But he'd apparently said "Fuck you" to that as well. She'd already chosen sides, he said. She'd abandoned Maude, after all Maude had done for her—looking out for her after her mother died, getting her the job at the library.

"I didn't need him to remind me of that," Prue said when she called to tell Maude about it.

"I know you didn't," was all Maude said in reply. Because of course both she and Prue knew well the compromises required in living out what was left of their lives as old and single women in the middle of the twentieth century. They'd spoken about it many times.

Besides, it was possible to exaggerate all that Maude had supposedly done for Prue. Though it's true that after she graduated from high school Prue had gone to secretarial school with Maude's encouragement. She might have encouraged Prue to go to college, but the girl was too shy to be a teacher and she needed money, not a husband. She'd lost her mother at around the age Maude had been when she lost hers.

⁎ ⁎ ⁎

NO ONE KNOWS EXACTLY where Tommy's been for the past year, since the day he learned that his sister was his mother. All anyone knows, now, is that he's enlisted in the Army. He'll leave for training camp in a week, he said when he called Maude. He wants to come see her one more time. He wants to sing some of the old songs with her, recite some of the old lines from Kipling. And he wants her to tell him stories about her life.

What he wants, Maude supposes, is one particular story. About the trip he took with her the summer when he a boy. To Cape May, New Jersey, and after that to Washington, DC. The trip that was perhaps the beginning of their end as an unusual sort of family. An unusual sort of family that had worked, for a time.

Well, she might say to him, he knew how much she was drinking back then. How could he expect her to remember?

But of course she remembers. The things both of them saw on that trip. What Prue had told him. Surely the real reason his grandmother Rose had insisted that he move into her house.

⁎ ⁎ ⁎

THE LETTER FROM ANNIE arrived in the spring.

Will you remember me, I wonder? was the first line of the letter.

Maude had laughed out loud when she read it. Then she'd covered her mouth and begun to weep.

The last twenty years of my life, since my children have stopped needing or wanting me, have been ones of unbroken misery, Annie wrote. *If you remember, if you can find it in your heart to care for me still, would you consider coming to visit—in the summer, when I'll be at the shore?* That was the last line of the letter. Maude bought a train ticket that day. The next day she changed the route—adding a stop in Washington—and bought a second ticket. That one was for Tommy. Because when Prue said, incredulously, you're going where? And what about Tom? Maude had replied without thinking, "I'll take him with me."

In Philadelphia, at the 30th Street Station, a driver with a car arrived to take them to the shore. Annie had a suite at the Congress Hotel in Cape May; she shared it with her daughter Liliane, a sly and secretive young woman with a lazy eye and a limp. Annie's son Robert, along with his wife and six-year-old son—a spoiled and sniffling towhead who followed Tommy around like a desperate puppy—were in the suite next to hers. When Maude and Tommy showed up that morning in late July, suitcases in tow, Robert took one look at them and left to arrange a room on the other side of the inn.

They stayed just short of a week, and each day was, for Maude, a blurry repetition of the one before. Everyone began drinking at noon—everyone, that is, but Annie's daughter Liliane, who mostly sat in the shadows, indoors or out, and observed. To Maude's eye there wasn't much to see. A bit of listless croquet on the lawn, some complaining about the heat, and then the incessant sniping and bickering between Annie and her son, which began during the cocktail hour and only ended when Annie rose, with Liliane's help, from her specially made chair on the verandah and collapsed into her bed for the night. Always before dinner, which Maude ate, each night, alone, in a hidden corner of the dining room.

Tommy, fortunately, had made fast friends with the grandchildren of Maxwell Milford's other family, from his first marriage, to the woman before Annie. By the second day of their stay he was off with them, to the boardwalk and the beach, and by that second night he'd asked if he could please sleep over at his new friends' rooms—in yet another group of suites elsewhere in the hotel. They'd arrived, it seemed, for the Milford Pharmaceuticals heirs' annual summer gathering, held each July in the patriarch's beloved resort hotel, the Chicago and Philadelphia branches together—children of Maxwell's two wives. He'd lived for less than ten years as husband to Annie, the second of those wives. She had raised the two children, Robert and Liliane, herself, in a house on Philadelphia's Main Line, soon regaining all the weight she'd lost to suit her husband's wishes, drinking steadily, and institutionalized, more than once. At least if her daughter Liliane was to be believed.

Each night, Robert matched his mother drink for drink, as did his wife. And then he would goad Annie into a fight, not content until she'd dissolved in tears. Liliane, in her conservative house dresses, generally found a rocker on the verandah and buried her head in a book. But, Maude saw, she watched everything closely. Liliane missed nothing.

Maude was relieved that Tommy had other things to do—away from Robert's whining six-year-old, away from the drunken adults. For the first few days, Maude held her own; she'd been a drinker too, of course, when she was younger. This is why the week was mostly a blur. And absolutely nothing like she'd expected, or hoped for, because Annie was no longer the Annie she'd known. She had kissed Maude absently, vaguely, only once—on the evening she and Tommy arrived. Her breath had reeked of smoke and rye. Her face was badly made up, powder cracking at the corners of her mouth and eyes, her hair dyed an unnatural black that nearly matched the color of Maude's own back in the days when she'd dyed it. Back in the days when she was Mick and The Bogus Man.

"Don't you remember those days?" Maude asked Annie once, on the third or fourth afternoon they were in Cape May. They were seated on the private verandah of Annie and Liliane's suite. The sun was low, but still hot; the wide lawn blazed before them, already turning brown. Beyond that was the ocean.

Annie stared at Maude blankly. She said nothing.

"You wrote to me back in May," Maude went on. "You wanted to know if I remembered you, if I recalled our days at the Gem."

But she stopped then, because Annie's head was listing to the side, her eyes drooping, a thin string of drool coursing over the powdery pink of her chin. And at that moment Maude had to admit that at age seventy her beloved Annie, her one great love, had become monstrous. Monstrous, repugnant even. She was gone from Maude for good.

Liliane had put her book down and was looking at Maude.

"May was before her last treatment," Liliane said as Maude rose from her chair and walked unsteadily toward the steps that led down to the lawn. Maude had stopped short, confused, at first, about who was speaking. "She won't remember anything about writing a letter to you," Liliane went on. Maude grasped the railing and turned to look at her. "The shock treatments relieve her of her memories, at least for a time. They tell us it's a blessing."

Liliane had kept her finger inside her book, Maude noticed, marking her place. Now she opened it and returned to reading.

It was the most Maude would hear Liliane say about her mother the entire time she was with the Milfords at Cape

May. And how was Maude to take those remarks, from that sneaking girl who was no longer a girl, who sat in silent judgment of them all, saying nothing? As pity? As pride? As both?

Maude would never know. That evening Robert stopped her on her way into the dining room. He had Tommy with him, washed and scrubbed, his wet hair slicked and combed behind his sunburned ears. It was probably best they leave the next morning, Robert said to her. He'd arranged a car for them at eight.

Tommy had moped for most of the train ride to Washington, angry at being dragged away from the beach and his new friends. But he'd brightened a bit at seeing the White House, then more at the Lincoln Memorial. For two days they'd walked to monuments and museums, and on their last morning she'd told him they were going to see another old friend.

* * *

PERHAPS THAT'S WHAT young Tom will want to ask her about now. About that taxi ride to St. Elizabeth's Hospital, where they'd joined the many others who'd come to see the great poet holding court in his room. She'd identified herself as a friend from his days as a professor at the college in Indiana.

His wife, dressed entirely in black, sat in the corner of the room, knitting silently. Some beatnik was reading something aloud from *The Washington Post* and raving about McCarthy. Also there was a barely dressed woman with long red hair, half hidden behind an easel where she was, apparently, painting the poet's portrait.

I do remember you, yes, he'd told her. Though you've aged, as we all have.

He unwrapped a sandwich, took a bite, and said "Will you join us for lunch?"

At that Maude shook her head. They couldn't stay, she said; they had to get to their train. But before they left Washington she'd simply wanted to see him, she said. And to ask him why he had done it.

The beatnik stopped reading and the wife's knitting needles stopped clicking and the scantily clad woman peered around her canvas.

The poet squinted up at her then, trying to read something in her face.

Why had he taken her in on those nights all those years ago? Was that what she was asking?

"No," she said. "That isn't it."

There was a strained silence in the room, a nervous waiting for what Maude might say next, and she had to admit she enjoyed that. She enjoyed making them all wait and wonder if she'd have the gall to ask.

She was simply curious, she said when she finally spoke, as to why he'd said those things on the radio, during the war, why he'd turned out to be like all the others.

Why, when he was such a gifted poet, he had needed to rail on about gold and the banks and all the things that men with no talent like his, with no imagination at all, spent all of their time talking about.

She had been at the mercy of men like that for her entire life, she continued. She'd pranced and sung for dimes in rooms full of fat-bellied men, then taken dictation and corrected the grammar of a man half her age, for thirty years, till he'd forced her out of the job the minute she turned sixty-five. She knew all she needed to know about money, and that was *not* what she went to poetry for.

What she could have used, she told him, was a bit more beauty. A bit more beauty without all the raving, without all the claptrap about money and gold and social credit theory, without all those ridiculous reminders of the very thing that had ruled, and mostly ruined, the better part of her life.

Where had it all come from that day, this string of complaints about his book? She had no idea. She hadn't known she was going to St. Elizabeth's to say such things. She hadn't known why she'd gone there at all.

At some point the beatnik had risen from his chair, reached for her arm, and tried to turn her toward the door. She should probably be on her way, he said. She'd made her speech and now she should go.

Then, to her surprise, Tommy was beside her, pulling the man's hand off her arm.

"Get your fuckin' hand off my Non," he said, his lip curled in an angry snarl.

As they walked down the long hallway, back to their waiting taxi, Tommy had asked her who the old man really was. "He didn't seem like a friend exactly," he said.

"That's true," she had answered. "He wasn't."

Then, as he opened the taxi door for her, Tommy asked, "Were you in love with him?"

She turned to look at him, shocked by the question. Too much time with those Milford step-cousins, she thought; that had to be it. Too many randy, foul-mouthed teenagers among them. She should have kept a closer eye on the boy.

"No. I was not."

"Just with her then? With fat old Mrs. Milford?"

Maude's breath had caught in her throat at that. Not at seeing the famous old poet. Not at being ushered from his room. Not even at hearing how Tommy spoke, the spitefulness in his words and his gestures as they left.

But at realizing that Tommy knew she'd once been in love with Annie.

In the taxi she'd asked, "Where'd you get an idea like that? From those Milford children was it?"

Tommy had stared hard at her for a moment, then turned to look out the window of the cab. He seemed to shake his head, but he didn't answer her.

Once on the train, though, he'd told her. The Milford cousins had all talked and laughed about it, yes. But he'd learned about it from Prue. "Prue said you were in love with her a long time ago."

. . .

TOM DOES SHOW UP for a visit five days after his phone call. It's the middle of the afternoon on the day before he'll "ship out," in his words, and he's as drunk as a sailor on leave. He doesn't stay long, and they don't sing songs or recite any Kipling. When she asks what he remembers about that long-ago trip east and whether he wants to ask her anything about the Milfords, or about that strange trip to St. Elizabeth's, he waves her questions away. He hardly remembers any of it, he says.

Is he nervous at all, about being in the Army? Maude asks him. It might be the only honest thing he says that day when he answers her. "Maybe a bit," he says.

"Don't make a mess of your life just to spite Rose, to get back at your grandmother," she tells him before he leaves. "She was only trying to do what she thought was best for you."

THE DIME MUSEUM

Tom nods. "The same for Prue and me," she adds.

Tom nods again, then hugs her and leaves, and when he's gone, Maude senses that she will not see him again. It is strange really, and also quite wonderful, she realizes at that moment, how expansive love can be, how well beyond what the ones who make the rules ("Family is everything") will tell you.

Maude rises from her chair to look for a book from the narrow shelf below her window: the Whitman. It isn't there, and she knows immediately that Tom has taken it. Well, good for him, she thinks. He'll need it, wherever he ends up. She closes her eyes and recalls the lines she wanted to read, still etched in her memory unlike the many other things she's forgotten: *Missing me one place search another, / I stop somewhere waiting for you.* Then she hums the melody of "After the Ball" until she drifts into sleep, sitting in the warmth of the afternoon sun that pours through her little window.

A Mind of Winter

PHILADELPHIA, 2012

I WOULD NEVER BE BEAUTIFUL. I knew this from a young age. Hence my experiment with the tall and comely Nina and her son. I have always been a careful observer, since well before my studies in the social sciences at the University of Pennsylvania. In this case, I would be a participant as well. I had a role to play.

Years before, I had found and read my mother's letters from a lost love, all of them in a satin pouch at the back of a drawer in her room. I was too young to understand them then, to grasp the coded language. The writer of the letters was called Mack, with the name enclosed in quotation marks. I was twelve when I first found and read them, and of course I made certain assumptions. My mother did not disabuse me of these, when she was cogent enough to talk with me about them.

"He was a young actor then?" I asked her. She'd appeared with him on the stage? And was he terribly handsome?

A strange smile when I asked her that, demure but devious.

"Oh yes, certainly," she told me. "Remarkably handsome. In a delicate, somewhat fragile way."

"And did you answer his letters? Even though Papa was still alive then? It sounds as if you broke his heart. What did you write back to him?"

"I didn't respond," she said. Though years later, in the weeks before a treatment (a time when she was always reckless, and often dangerous), she did write back. I've wondered if I somehow put the idea in her head all those years before. Some grandiosity there, I suppose. What I did or said seldom registered with my mother.

In any case, I thought what afflicted me might have been true for Nina as well—a mother's lack of interest, I mean. Hers was perhaps too busy with the household, the failing farm, to bother with a daughter. Or this was my picture of the situation, though I never probed. I encouraged Nina to write to her mother nonetheless, to send pictures of her grandson. At some point I thought I would arrange a visit by her mother to my home in Philadelphia, where Nina and her son Charlie were living. But before I managed to do so, Nina's mother was dead.

My mother's death was equally unceremonious and happened shortly after her visit from "Mack"—who, it turned out, was a woman. And was I surprised? I suppose I was. It saddened me, honestly, watching the eager thing, whose real name was Maude. Mother had had her treatment a week before Maude arrived with a mysterious grandson in tow. Only once or twice, throughout Maude's brief stay, did my mother give the slightest sign of even recognizing her.

To be beautiful I would have needed to start with my weak knee and my limp from polio, perhaps. Then there was my right eye, whose motions I could not control. Yet what would have been the point? My hair is limp and dull. I lean toward heaviness, like both my mother and my father. My heart and lungs are weak, though not so weak as either of theirs had been. I inherited neither of my parents' love of drink and laughter, something they shared in the early years of their marriage at least, before my father died and my mother began to drink until she was raving. Back then I disputed few, if any, of my father's previous family members' recommendations. And, in fact, it was my brother, her own son, who insisted on the electro-shock treatments.

I was distracted by my own life at the time, sunk in the years of mourning my one and only love. At the age of seventeen I'd enrolled at the University of Pennsylvania. The American literature courses I took there were taught by a brilliant man named William Sharpless. He was young, a new faculty member. He was blond and fair, delicate, almost feminine. I loved him, and he knew this, and he did not dissuade me. I suppose I seemed eminently safe.

"Your readings are astute," he told me after class one day.

He'd just returned my analysis of Part V of *The Waste Land*. Eliot's language had washed over me as I read in the quiet of midnight, flooding me with longing, making me lean my head on the windowsill to still my pounding heart. The poet's every word somehow signaled, and magnified, my own yearning. And I craved every brilliant utterance from William Sharpless's soft and sensual mouth. His words flowed alongside the music of Eliot's lines, one beautiful river flowing along, and through, the other.

"—unlike others in the class," William added that day. Who seemed, he said, to respond to Eliot with a collective shudder of despair and contempt. Not to mention a maddening lack of understanding, despite his lectures.

And another time: "You mustn't be fearful, Liliane. Your reading and your ideas are sound. Ignore the ones who say you don't belong here." He meant my family. He knew immediately who the Milfords were. By then the success of my father's pharmaceutical business had made him a Philadelphia magnate.

Once, on a quiet lawn behind the library, we sat together on a blanket, William and I, sipping tea from his thermos and reading. At one point he reached over and stroked my hair, absently, a single time. His eyes never left his book.

I marked the page I was reading that day with my own blood, from a needle-prick to my finger. I vowed never to say that poem's sacred name, a heartsick and childish vow that I have, nonetheless, honored to this day.

It was William Sharpless who introduced me to the American Modernists—mainly his favorites: Eliot, Pound, Stevens. Sometimes we read the poems together, aloud, in his office or on a bench behind the library, puzzling over them for hours. Time and time again we returned to his favorite, Stevens's "The Snow Man" ("One must have a mind of winter . . ."), which I loved as well, though I think for different reasons. Both of us thrilled to the starkness, the devastating purity, of Stevens's lines. The perfect mastery.

As we also thrilled to modern art, or some of it—Degas, Matisse, the challenges posed by Picasso—as we walked through the rooms of the Barnes Museum, rolling our eyes at the sloppy excess of some of Albert Barnes's chosen painters, the ridiculous, cluttered aspect of the walls, thanks to Barnes's idiosyncratic arrangements. Akin, I often thought, to his own loud and insolent life, the life of a poor man who'd grown rich. This was surely why he loved the dreadful work of a painter like the Jewish wastrel Soutine.

And yet other works in his collection filled me with— something. A kind of longing, for what I wasn't sure. Or a sense of somehow being known. De Chirico's "La meditazione del pomeriggio" grabbed me by the back of my prickling neck the first time I saw it, with William, on a chilly afternoon in March; it stopped me in my tracks. The hunched, exhausted man with his traveling case, frozen into a statue, perched in an empty square in the ruthless light of noon. The wind of a distant train passing him by. Alone there. Lost, forgotten, utterly despairing.

As we viewed it together I turned away so William would not see my tears. I was certain he and I were both thinking the same thing, which was that the man in the painting might have been our beloved Wallace Stevens. Or either one of us. Trapped within and bewildered, yet also enthralled, by modernity.

William must have sensed my feeling, and he reached for my hand. He turned to me, and he kissed me, softly, on the cheek.

After that, he avoided me, claiming to be busy reading, or grading, when I knocked on his office door. This went on for a month, more, and I thought at the time that I was as sad and forlorn as I could ever possibly be.

Perhaps all the time I spent in his office or walking with him on the campus on warmer afternoons had offered him a kind of cover. For a time.

Later, I would go back to the work of Havelock Ellis, whom I'd read for a psychology of sexuality course. How scandalized my family would have been if they knew! I'd used only my first initial—so as to disguise my sex—and enrolled for that very reason. To shock my family (not that anyone was paying attention). And because I was curious.

Specifically, I returned to Ellis's chapter on sexual inversion. It hadn't quite registered the first time I read it, the capacity of sexual inversion to contribute to the purification of man. To eliminate, through the absence of procreation, unworkable urges.

I could have loved William Sharpless in a pure and uncomplicated way, if only I'd had the chance to do so. I could have suppressed any residual urges I might have had by then, of this I was certain. I'd begun doing so long before, at the age of seven in fact, when a nanny came into my room and discovered me pleasuring myself with a pillow that I held between my legs. She caned both my hands and bottom for that, followed by a scalding hot bath and soap rubbed inside me until I was raw. Pleasure of that sort meant pain, I learned from my nanny, and I have always been uniquely sensitive, and averse, to pain.

I could have loved and cared for William Sharpless had he only let me. Had he not succumbed to the wiles of another faculty member, the married man who'd taught my introductory anthropology course, in whose office William Sharpless was discovered, in a state of undress and spent passion, by a bewildered first-year student near the end of my second year at the university.

* * *

MY BROTHER ROBERT and his wife produced a son who was at first a whining and sniveling child, then a brutal and greedy adult. He married a beautiful woman, however, and they in turn produced a strikingly handsome but rather derelict son, my grand-nephew Michael, who should have been monitored more closely and steered toward a better college, Haverford at a minimum. But his parents were too distracted, and both died young. He enrolled at a large and innocuous state university, where all was not lost, because that is where he met, and impregnated, the lovely Nina. The beautiful, blank slate at the heart of my experiment.

They produced an equally attractive child, Charlie, who seems to have inherited his father's lack of motivation in school and grades that do not reflect his promise. Presumably he also inherited some unfortunate propensities from Nina's side, though she's shared little about her family with me through the years. So here I am, unfortunately, relying mainly on speculation: the poor, part-time farmer and part-time coal miner father, the embittered Midwestern wife, the lie-about brothers. I've been able to draw my own conclusions. It is not my habit to probe or pry; I merely observe.

Give the boy time, I told Nina on several occasions. Keep him in private schools, and all will be well in the end.

Though it *is* concerning that all the boy seems interested in is the game of basketball and the loudly recited lyrics of the songs of angry black men.

I had never experienced such despair as I felt in the face of William's obvious avoidance of me, following his chaste kiss on my cheek. But I could, and would, sink into a deeper, and lasting, despondency six weeks later, when the student who discovered him in the anthropology professor's office spoke to the dean. And when, two days later, William Sharpless put a gun to his head and died.

Though nearly ten years had passed, I had scarcely recovered from the shock of William's suicide when Maude arrived for her strange visit. Then, shortly afterwards, my mother died. My days were empty after Annie's death. What was left for me then? I could have returned to my studies, I suppose, but to what end? And so for years I read poetry, and I began secretly writing poems on my own. I had no guidance, and no clear aim. But once, in a fit of hubris, I mailed a poem to the poet Ezra Pound, shortly before the end of his stay at St. Elizabeth's Hospital, a place where my mother had stayed on more than one occasion, hidden from the prying eyes of wealthy Philadelphians. Perhaps that was what had made me so bold.

I've no idea what I expected. It honestly shames me now, to think of it—my youthful naivete, my reckless belief in my own talent. Pound must have recognized something that merited encouragement, however—or perhaps caught a hint of my wealth? (Though I'd used a pseudonym to avoid that.) He told me in no uncertain terms that my poem was not good. But, he wrote, this was no reason not to continue reading poetry, and trying to write more. He recommended subscribing to a magazine I did not know of, an obscure and struggling one, produced in Chicago.

This set me on a journey that would last more than thirty years, until Nina's arrival and even beyond, maneuvering my way into a leadership role at the charitable foundation at my father's company, despite my brother's strong objections. The children of my father's first marriage feared a lawsuit; I'd made veiled threats. For years I attended board meetings faithfully, only listening and observing. Again, a born anthropologist. Not attempting to shape any policy or funding decision. At first.

Until the circumstances were right. Until I had wormed my way near the top and could make decisions of my own. The board, and the rest of the Milford family, be damned.

Once again it seemed they barely noticed me or my actions. They had bigger fish to fry—that is, the company and its fortunes. Evading lawsuits, and of course tax laws, that sort of thing. No one cared, really, about the foundation. I could do with that money what I would.

And so I handed that obscure Chicago magazine, still hanging on nearly thirty years after I began reading it, a gift of fifty million dollars. No strings attached.

They didn't even have to publish my work—which of course I'd never sent them. One rebuff from Ezra Pound was enough. I knew my place.

And by that time I had other work to do. Constructing a nursery in my house, interviewing a series of nannies. Training Nina in the intricacies of being the kind of elite Philadelphian I had been in name only. She had the additional gift of beauty. There would be no stopping her, I assumed. I could spend my days reading, swimming in my pool, and continuing to write, in secret. The rest would be up to her.

I observed—both Nina and Charlie, mother and son—and I kept notes. Monitoring my other legacy, controlling what I could. Soon after Charlie's birth I urged Nina to get her perfect body back. I gifted her a lifetime membership at my club for that purpose, hired yoga teachers and trainers for her. I took her to charity benefits, cocktail parties and dinners, all of it so that she might meet equally wealthy and attractive men.

And then I observed her various relationships with distant interest. None of the men she dated, I realized, was likely to capture Nina's mysterious, impenetrable heart. I assume she enjoyed the sex, at least for a while. We did not speak of this.

Then the oncologist from Lisbon crossed her path, in the waning days of the Barnes Museum's life in its original home, the mansion in Lower Merion. They met at a lecture and benefit there—one that, unfortunately, I had urged her to attend with me. A widower with darkly handsome eyes, a tall and lithe frame, a quiet and seductive voice. His name was Silvio.

THE DIME MUSEUM

This set off alarm bells, for a brief time. I could see she was falling for him. And so I reminded her of something quite important in the widower Silvio's case: the children from his first marriage. One of them, a girl of twelve, had a spinal injury that had left her an invalid.

"Remember," I said to Nina casually one evening at cocktails, before she left for a date with Silvio during one of his visits to Philadelphia. "If you were to marry him, you would have to leave me. You would have to move to Lisbon. You would inherit all that comes with loving a man like that. Including his two children, one of them with very pronounced needs."

Needs that, I did not have to remind the lovely Nina, would be well beyond her capacities as a caretaker. She had no training and next to no experience in such matters. She'd needed neither, within the safe and comfortable confines of my experiment, my project of cultivating something essential. A delicate, flawless flower. Untarnished beauty. The purity of new snow.

A week later Nina told me she had ended her relationship with Silvio.

As I've said, mostly I have observed. Only at times, and when absolutely necessary, have I participated.

Only because it was for the best. Only to protect certain assets, and of course myself.

I could have loved William Sharpless, in a way that surely could have sufficed for us both. Had he only let me. Had he not succumbed, as so many do, to the strange and ungovernable urges of the human heart.

Winged Siren Seizing an Adolescent

LISBON, 2020

TESS AND HER CHILDREN meet the children's former nanny, Olivia, on a Friday in March. It's the end of Olivia's first week in a new job, an unusually warm day, the sun straining behind gray clouds. Lisbon never exactly gleams, except at the waterfront, but today the city seems to shimmer. Glancing in the windows they pass on the way to Olivia's office building, Tess sees her children reflected in a honeyed glow. They certainly aren't angels but they're good children, Tess thinks as she steers her brood—ten-year-old Ari, eight-year-old Ines, and three-year-old Esti—through the high glass entrance to Olivia's building. For a moment she experiences something that's been happening a lot lately, the strange feeling that she is seeing these children from a considerable distance. That they are somehow not her own.

She recalls her earliest days in Portugal, pushing Amalia's wheelchair over the narrow sidewalks, riding the elevator with her to the top of the Amoreiras shopping center. Back then, Tess was the age Olivia had been when she arrived in Lisbon, twenty-two. She was also at the beginning of a life, a life like a story, one she never would have imagined for herself.

Silvio, her husband, assumed she'd been named after Tess of the D'Urbervilles, the character in the Hardy novel. He'd lived his entire life in Portugal but had read more English novels than she had. She'd never heard of it, she told him, too young and naïve to lie. Tess was just a nickname her Irish grandmother had given her, short for Teresa. Back then, she'd told Silvio everything. She'd seen no reason to lie. She wasn't out to impress him; she was his employee.

As soon as they enter the building, an elevator opens and Olivia emerges. And while Tess feels many things on seeing her in this unfamiliar context, mostly she is troubled by the girl's dress.

She isn't a girl, Tess knows this, but for the moment that's the only word that fits. The dress Olivia has worn to work on this day, a striped orange-red Missoni sundress from ten years before, had until recently belonged to Tess. Olivia had spotted it in her closet on her final day with the family two weeks ago, when Tess invited her to go through her things. She was nervous about not having the right wardrobe for her new job at an architecture firm in the heart of Lisbon.

"It's gorgeous," Olivia breathed that morning, her big brown eyes even wider than usual, when she pulled the dress from the recesses of Tess's closet. Tess had actually forgotten about that dress, though she could have still worn it; ten years and three children later, she was basically the same size. And it *was* a stunning dress: intricate knitwear, form-fitting at the waist and the low-cut bodice, with a softly gathered skirt. It had been a gift from Silvio.

For a moment that morning, while Olivia held the dress aloft on its padded hanger, Tess had allowed herself to savor the memory of how various men—Silvio, his brothers, his colleagues from the hospital—had looked at her when she wore it. Once at a cocktail party, she remembered, and another time at a gathering at the family compound at Cascais. The dress wasn't really her color, but it hadn't seemed to matter because she'd had a newfound glow that summer. She'd just learned that she was pregnant with Ari. Silvio had bought her the dress to celebrate.

"Take it," she'd said without thinking that morning. Or actually she *was* thinking something, which was that the dress would look infinitely better on Olivia, with her smooth young skin and her lush, dark brown hair, than it had ever looked against Tess's pale, freckled arms and her head of unruly red hair. Glowingly pregnant or not.

Silvio had loved that dress on her, and she'd loved wearing it for him. But Olivia would have many more opportunities to wear it now, Tess told herself as she pulled more hangers from the closet for Olivia's perusal, barely noticing what was on them.

That day, it was mostly self-pity Tess was nursing. Olivia was leaving them, starting a whole new life apart from them. Tess was supposed to have started her own new life—a new plan, a new project—while Olivia took care of her children. But that was going nowhere.

So that was self-pity, but what is this? This feeling that's making her want to shake her head and pull Olivia aside, explain to her in a discreet whisper that the dress, while certainly beautiful on her, is surely wrong for work. Only a young and naïve girl would wear something like that to an office.

But Tess says nothing. Instead she smiles as her daughters run to Olivia, Esti jumping into her arms and Ines wrapping her arms around Olivia's waist.

For a moment Tess imagines Charlie, the blond American who'd come to spend last weekend with Olivia, admiring the dress. But instead of Olivia, she pictures Charlie admiring the dress on *her*. Admiring it, and then unzipping it. She shudders a little, then shakes away the pinch of pleasure the thought has given her, pushing bashful Ari forward and telling him to say hello to Olivia.

She's really still a kid herself, Tess thinks, watching her daughters treat Olivia like a piece of playground equipment. Even in that gorgeous, if wildly inappropriate, dress.

• • •

OLIVIA WORKED FOR THEM for a year and a half, caring for the children in the relaxed and open-hearted way that she seemed to do everything, from running to the market for something that Tess needed for dinner to cleaning up another stream of vomit from the family's aging cat. Her mother was Brazilian, so Olivia spoke Portuguese with an accent that made Ines laugh and made Ari, who had an obvious crush on his nanny, blush with pleasure. She'd grown up in a big, noisy household, the oldest of six children, and that had taught her the true meaning of multi-tasking and, she said, "not to sweat the small stuff." Tess had marveled at that, as someone whose entire life, until very recently, had been about accounting for, adding up, checking things off of various lists. Basically sweating every small thing.

Olivia was beautiful, and that might have been a threat. After all, Tess herself had been the nanny for Rafa and Amalia, Silvio's children from his first marriage, when she arrived in Lisbon in 2007.

Silvio's first wife had died of ovarian cancer three years before Tess arrived, a particularly trying death for the wife of a prominent oncologist. Rafa was eleven and Amalia was nine when she died, but a year later Amalia suffered a traumatic brain injury in a skiing accident, and after that she needed round-the-clock care. Silvio had tried relying on day nurses and handling his children's care on his own at night, until his brothers had performed a kind of intervention, insisting he seek round-the-clock help and locating an international agency that placed nannies with skilled nursing credentials. Tess had just graduated from college in Philadelphia, with a nursing degree, when Silvio's oldest brother contacted her through that agency. She'd listed with them before she graduated, hoping for an adventure abroad.

Silvio was a loving, if distracted, father; he was devoted to his children, but even more devoted to his work. He had no time for romance, it seemed, and Tess was the one who finally asked him to kiss her. It was late on a cool October night, moonlight casting shadows in Silvio's darkened study, a breeze lifting the curtain at the floor-to-ceiling window. The flat, which occupied an entire floor of an early twentieth-century building in Santo António, was always warm; Silvio kept the windows cracked year-round.

They were both exhausted from the day, and from settling Amalia as comfortably as possible, her breathing tube in place and the pillows adjusted at her back, behind her knees and along the railing at the sides of her bed. Most nights, she and Silvio did this together, though Tess had quickly become adept at lifting Amalia's small body, carefully cradling her thin arms and legs. But when Silvio was home, not working late or traveling to some international conference or symposium, he always wanted to help.

If Silvio were a different sort of man, Tess might have blamed him for inviting her to join him in his study for a glass of scotch at the end of many of those long, tiring days.

But it was Tess who'd first acknowledged her desire for this tall and broodingly handsome man, this devoted father and renowned physician. Her employer.

"Would you kiss me?" she'd asked as he handed her her drink that night. He'd only hesitated for a moment before nodding, carefully setting his drink down and pulling her into his arms.

Before she fell in love with Silvio, Tess had come to love his children. Rafa with his long hair and ruddy cheeks, practicing soccer moves in the vast apartment's foyer, Amalia with her sad smile and searching eyes, her head, which seemed so large relative to the rest of her fragile body, lolling to the side.

This was not something she'd expected when she signed on to be a nurse/nanny abroad. She had not imagined being able to love anyone's children in that way. She'd studied nursing, not education—which her mother, herself a nurse, had urged her to pursue instead. And unlike many of her friends in the nursing program Tess hadn't found ill or injured children any sadder, any more worthy of her diligent care, than any other patients she'd encountered on her clinical rotations. Pediatrics had been just another thing to check off her list.

She'd assumed this work with Silvio's children would feel the same—a cool, detached, routine. She'd expected to be good at it, competent and diligent, just as she'd been as a student. But Rafa and Amalia were so obviously their father's children. Both had his sad, hooded eyes, his quiet and watchful presence. Both were gentle and kind.

She'd loved them almost immediately. And then, when she began having her own children with Silvio, the surge of love she'd felt had seemed, at times, like it might suffocate her. At first.

Before Olivia's arrival, before Tess had realized how little her children actually needed her. How invisible she was to them. To everyone really.

. . .

TESS'S DAUGHTERS ARE CLINGING to Olivia like eager monkeys. Ari has resisted Tess's nudge; he stands back, watching shyly through the fringe of his untamable hair. Tess clicks her tongue at the girls, peeling Esti's strong little arms from Olivia's neck.

"It's fine!" Olivia laughs, setting Esti down and stroking both girls' hair. "I'm so happy to see everyone." She steps closer to Ari and ruffles his hair too. "Time for a haircut, dude," she says. He smiles at her and nods, and Tess makes a mental note to schedule hair appointments for all three children. Another thing she'll need to remember now that Olivia's gone.

There's a bar in the lobby of this new office tower, and Tess orders tea for herself and for Olivia, hot chocolates for the children. Olivia settles everyone at a table set between the big front windows and a cluster of giant, unrecognizable plants in mosaic pots while Tess waits to pay. She watches Olivia chatting easily with the children, seeming to hardly notice as Esti climbs onto her lap. For some reason, Tess had pictured her in some sort of suit—stylish trousers and a jacket, though where Olivia would have gotten an outfit like that would have been anyone's guess. Certainly she wouldn't have found it in Tess's closet. And where had Tess gotten the idea in the first place? Probably something she'd seen in a magazine; where else would she have picked up ideas about how professional women were supposed to dress? Few of the women in Silvio's big, extended family worked outside their homes. The ones who did, the younger ones, did things involving the internet somehow—Tess never quite understood what. They seemed to dress mostly in leggings and expensive t-shirts.

She'd been picturing this meeting all week. Seeing Olivia in her Missoni dress has thrown her a bit, but otherwise it's begun pretty much as she imagined. She'll ask Olivia about her job while they drink their tea and then, when there's a moment that feels right, she'll ask about Charlie. Olivia met him on a trip she took during her holiday at New Year's. Tess knew little about their relationship; Olivia kept her personal life to herself.

To begin with, she'll ask, is he still in Lisbon? She's only curious, she'll say, as nonchalantly as possible, because of this worrisome new virus we're hearing about. There's reported to be an outbreak in Italy.

Tess knows it's worrisome because Silvio talks about it at night now, after dinner and after the children are in bed. Now Rafa lives and works in Los Angeles, and Amalia lives with other disabled adults in a state-of-the-art group home that Silvio co-founded. Ari and Ines put themselves to bed, requiring only quick kisses, and she and Silvio take turns reading to Esti until she finally settles into sleep. Then they chat a bit, sometimes, over their usual glasses of scotch. Though often these days, Tess says she's too tired and Silvio never seems to mind. He's always tired as well, but that never stops him from retreating to his study to work for a couple more hours, catching up on patient files, reading journal articles.

It's worse than anyone realizes, Silvio said two nights ago as they yawned over their drinks. In Italy—particularly in the north—it's becoming especially bad.

• • •

BESIDES CARING FOR HIS CHILDREN, Silvio and Tess had shared an interest in the art collection of Albert Barnes. But how was this possible? she'd asked him on the night they made this discovery, soon after her arrival in Lisbon. Other than some artists and art historians, it had seemed to Tess that no one outside of Philadelphia had even heard of Albert Barnes.

Silvio had smiled and nodded, acknowledging this. It was "purely an accident," he said, and she'd repeated the phrase to herself—then and later—relishing his accented English, the purring softness of it. He'd been at the University of Pennsylvania for a conference years ago, and a friend had taken him to an event at the Barnes Museum.

Tess had added up the years, amazed and delighted. "That would have been the original museum then?" she said. "Were you in the house in Lower Merion?"

Yes, he'd been there. It was a fundraising event, he said, connected with plans for the new building in Center City. Something for private donors. "I learned that night that not everyone was pleased about the plans for a new building," Silvio had said. "Perhaps you know more about this?"

Remarkably, she did know. At last there was *something* that Tess could tell him about (even his knowledge of bedside patient care usually surpassed, hers). Despite being a working-class Irish Catholic girl from the Philly suburbs, she had, for a bright but fleeting moment, considered majoring in art. This had everything to do with the collector Albert Barnes, with his eclectic and fraught collection of European paintings and African masks and Pennsylvania Dutch stoneware and barn door hinges and old tools.

She'd gone to the original museum once, when she was fifteen, Tess told Silvio that night. "I fell in love with it. Everything about it really, especially the Modigliani paintings." She went on to tell him about her art minor in college, how she'd mainly studied art history but had also taken a few classes in drawing and painting, whatever she could fit in alongside the crowded nursing requirements. She didn't tell him that she'd thought, once, about changing her major. She didn't tell him that what had stopped her was the obvious reality that art was, in fact, for the wealthy. No matter what Albert Barnes might have imagined for his private collection. After all, look how that had turned out.

Only a man with Albert Barnes's fortune could imagine a world in which poor and working-class people had the time and luxury to learn about, and appreciate, art. That had been her mother's reaction, when Tess visited the original Barnes Museum on a high school field trip and told her mother about it afterwards. By that time her mother had finished her own degree, a B.S. in Nursing, slowly ticking off the necessary classes year after year, and she'd finally been promoted to head nurse on the surgical step-down floor she'd worked on for years.

Her mother was tired, bone-tired, all the time, and every night she soaked her feet after dinner. She'd developed some sort of neuropathy, she assumed—chronic tingling and pain. But who had time, she said, to seek an actual diagnosis?

From her mother, Tess had learned her own detached yet laser-focused way of attending to patients. "All care, zero need." This was what her mother told the nurses who worked on her floor. Except for pausing for drinks of water and emptying their bladders (and the less of the former the better, to make for less of the latter), for the eight hours of their shifts they were to be entirely about the care and tending of others. Not themselves.

But then, the one detail Tess knew about her mother's teenage years was that she'd thought seriously about becoming a nun. *All care, zero need.* It made complete sense for her mother.

Her mother took care of everything, and she never complained, and she did not understand people who *did* complain. If Tess had told her that she'd decided to study art, her mother would have taken that in stride, with little, if any, commentary. But still Tess would have recognized the added weight on her mother's tired back, the heightened pain in her feet. The additional worry scoring her exhausted face.

Tess's father left when her brother was four and she was two. Her brother graduated from high school and enlisted in the Air Force, and after that they saw him maybe once a year, at Christmas time. Tess did well in high school and got a healthy scholarship to the small college where her mother had completed her own degree only a couple of years before.

After college would come work, and paying off her loans. Ticking things off her list. Little did she know she'd end up married to her first employer, a man who'd made all the zeros in the college debt she'd carried with her to Portugal disappear with one call to his accountant.

Her drink, and her fatigue, were making her too chatty, she thought that night in Silvio's study years ago. And what would she do if he asked her more about her interest in art, about early modern painting, about the theory of education in art appreciation that Albert Barnes had developed in partnership with John Dewey? That bit about loving the work of Modigliani, for instance—that had been a bit of a stretch.

And why would this accomplished and sophisticated older man, this successful physician whose children she'd been hired to tend to, even care? Yet she knew she wasn't imagining a new light of interest in his eyes.

Later, she would tell him that in fact she knew nothing about art when she enrolled in an art history course to fulfill a college requirement. That she'd been on exactly one school trip to the Philadelphia Art Museum as a child—and remembered nothing but the famous stairs to the main entrance—when, in high school, she had boarded the bus for another school trip to the old Barnes Museum on Philadelphia's Main Line.

The boys from her school had moved quickly and noisily through the high-ceilinged rooms of the museum that day, snickering at the fleshy, busty women in all the Renoirs and at Courbet's bare-assed *Woman with White Stockings*, daring the viewer to look away from her exposed crotch as she pulls on her sock. Tess had hung back as her friends strolled more languidly through the rooms, mostly talking, only occasionally glancing up at walls covered in what Tess would later come to understand were odd and disjointed combinations of paintings, sculptures, craftwork. Pairings and groupings shaped by Albert Barnes's own idiosyncratic logic. For some reason, she'd wanted to experience those rooms, that entire mansion, on her own.

She wished she could say that it was the art that had made her private and pensive that day—moody, silent, somehow constantly on the cusp of tears. She *had* stopped short on reaching the room that held a Modigliani painting called *Redheaded Girl in Evening Dress* at the center of the wall. What drew Tess to that painting were the woman's skinny arms and long neck and her pile of red hair, rather like Tess's own. The redheaded girl was surrounded by paintings of squat women and hip-heavy nudes and a peculiar circus acrobat, all of them in much smaller paintings by an artist, Picasso, who Tess had actually heard of. The redheaded girl looked bored, she thought, bored and unimpressed by all the treasures Barnes had selected to surround her with. Bored and insolent. Tess had admired her.

For some reason, she connected the red-haired woman in the painting with the one truly arresting and memorable event of that day—something that had happened in the parking lot before they even entered the museum. Only a set number of people could enter the museum at a time, and her high school group had been granted access ahead of a bus full of students from a private, Catholic school in the suburban town next to theirs—a school she and her classmates knew well, one the rich kids from their town attended. Walking to the entrance that day, they could see those kids in their blue uniform blazers, the boys wearing ties that they'd loosened at their necks, their faces pressed against the bus's fogged-over windows, watching Tess and her classmates walk into the museum. For a moment she realizes—and it's funny, but not really surprising to recognize this—that Olivia's Charlie had reminded her of those boys, and others like them she'd known, peripherally, when she was young. Blond and beautiful, full of swagger. Confident in a way she knew she'd never be.

The private school bus driver kept the engine running, presumably to keep the heat on. They'd have to wait, one of Tess's teachers said, because their driver hadn't followed the rules; he'd entered the parking lot the wrong way and before their allotted time. In fact, they'd be lucky, the teacher said, if they got in at all that day.

Tess had felt a strange mix of exhilaration and shame when she heard that. Shame for the private school kids who'd gotten it wrong, or maybe for their poor bus driver, but also exhilaration that she and her classmates—the children of cops and nurses and plumbers and public school teachers— had gotten it right. That they were walking ahead of those rich private school kids, in full view, entering the mansion while those kids could only watch from inside the overheated prison of their bus.

Years later, Tess took an art history class with Les, the adjunct professor who would become her mentor in college. One day at office hours she told him about that field trip. Les said that what she witnessed that day was just the sort of thing Albert Barnes had had in mind for his museum.

"You and your classmates were the kind of visitors he wanted to influence, to teach about art," he said, shoving a pile of blue books aside to make room for his giant coffee mug. Les's office was in the social sciences building because he was a lawyer who mainly taught night classes on law and society. But he'd also been part of the group of Barnes disciples who were trained in the collector's distinctive method of art appreciation and education. She wasn't sure Les had ever actually practiced law. But he was passionate in his view that the Philadelphia philanthropists who'd insisted they were "rescuing" the Barnes collection by building the new museum in Center City had brazenly defied the explicit instructions in Albert Barnes's will. Les's students got to hear about that in pretty much every lecture he delivered.

She *should* have asked him how he could possibly know what a dead art collector would have thought about her and her classmates, most of whom were bored to tears by the Barnes collection and couldn't wait to get to McDonald's for lunch. But instead, she had basked in Les's weird approval of her and her background. Why hadn't she simply said to him, *You know absolutely nothing about me?*

WHEN THEIR DRINKS ARE READY, Olivia jumps from the table to help Tess carry everything. She's added pastries to occupy the children; they'll be bored within minutes, or Esti will be anyway, and Tess wants time to chat with Olivia. To hear about her week, to get a sense of how the new job is going; Silvio will want to know. And to ask about Charlie.

Esti follows Olivia, holding onto her hand. Watching them walk to the table ahead of her, Tess can understand why people have sometimes thought Olivia was Esti's mother. All of Tess and Silvio's children have their father's darker complexion, and Ines and Esti got his dark hair as well. Only Ari has reddish-blond hair, curly like Tess's and perpetually in his eyes. Tess watches him furtively watching Olivia from his seat at the table, where he's pretending to do something on his phone. And she wonders if he has any memory of his mother wearing that dress.

"The work is wonderful," Olivia says. The firm she's working for does sustainable architecture, the thing she'd studied in the U.S., at Syracuse.

"It's perfect, and I'm learning so much. Please thank Silvio for me again."

Tess nods absently, cutting Esti's pastry into bite-size pieces. She tries to look nonchalant as she asks, "And how is your friend? How is Charlie?"

Olivia could have continued to live with them; they had room, and they'd offered—at least until she'd been at the job for a while, until she could comfortably look for a place of her own. Instead she'd contacted Charlie, who was what exactly? Friend, lover, both, something else? *Fuck-buddy* had been Silvio's niece Claudia's word for it, and in her accented English it sounded friendly and playful. All of Silvio's sisters and sisters-in-law, and their grown daughters, spoke about sex in an amused, offhand way. Affairs were taken for granted, on both their partners' part and their own. They teased Tess about her innocence and devotion; Silvio, they said, had found the only other saint in Lisbon to marry when he hired Tess. They were merciless when Olivia arrived, and yet Tess had never worried. Because Silvio was a saint? Probably. Maybe. Though how can anyone ever be sure?

She could only know the truth about herself at this point. Claudia had also introduced her to the term MILF. A *mom I'd like to fuck*.

"Keep an eye on this guy when he arrives," she'd said. "He might turn to you next, Tess. You might be his MILF."

Much as she hates to admit it, that's probably where Tess had gotten the idea.

· · ·

OLIVIA HAD MET HIM on holiday in Venice. He had a place to stay in Lisbon, an apartment in the Principe Real that was mostly empty, belonging to someone he knew, his to use whenever he wanted apparently. He came to spend the weekend with Olivia before she started her new job. She'd packed her bags and taken everything—Tess's Missoni dress included—along to Principe Real last Friday.

Olivia doesn't seem surprised by the question. Or maybe she seems amused. Tess can't quite read her face.

"I assume he's fine," she says. "He left on Tuesday."

But you're living in his apartment, Tess thinks, then wonders, does a free apartment often go along with being fuck-buddies? Is it a kind of incentive?

"He had a cough, I noticed," she says. "When you brought him to the apartment to meet the children last Friday."

Now Olivia looks puzzled. "He did? I'm sorry. I wasn't aware of that."

Tess waves her hand. "No, no need to be sorry." And then she remembers that yes, of course: she'd noticed his cough on Monday. Not on Friday, not the day he arrived in Lisbon and came to the apartment to pick up Olivia and help her with her bags. Tess had insisted that Olivia invite him in, and he'd charmed the children. And Tess as well.

He was blond and tall and muscular, his arms etched with intricate and colorful tattoos that fascinated Esti, who couldn't keep her hands off him. He hadn't seemed to mind. Tess feels a twinge of worry at the memory but then reminds herself that Silvio said that the virus isn't an issue for children. They seem not to be particularly susceptible.

They'd discussed where Charlie and Olivia might have dinner that evening. Tess suggested a Goan restaurant that they all loved. He said he liked Indian food but hadn't had food from that region.

"The one area colonized by Portugal," Tess explained. "Of course," he'd said. They talked more about Italy, about Portuguese attitudes about migrants as compared to Italian attitudes. This topic interested him; he grew animated, engaged in a way Olivia never was when Tess brought up Brexit, the political situation in the U.S., really anything beyond the bounds of the children's lives and their needs.

Somehow it emerged that he'd attended college in a town not far from the Philadelphia suburb Tess was from. When he told her his last name she'd laughed; it was a well-known name in Philadelphia but, she assumed, probably his was a different family. When she said "Oh, like the pharmaceuticals company?" though, he'd said, "Actually, yes," then hurried to change the subject. And Tess thought that that at least explained a mostly unused and readily available apartment in the Principe Real.

The more she and Charlie talked last Friday, the more visibly restless Olivia became. She seemed bored by their conversation and eager to leave. It dawned on Tess then that Olivia was probably eager to bed him. At realizing this, she'd felt a kind of power. Charlie actually seemed in no particular hurry to leave. He was clearly enjoying talking with her. Even if Olivia was his actual fuck-buddy.

* * *

ON MONDAY, Olivia's first day at her new job, Tess had taken Esti to stay with Silvio's youngest sister after Ari and Ines left for school. Then she'd gone to the salon. And then to the Goan restaurant she'd mentioned, to buy food for lunch. And she'd taken it to the apartment where Charlie was staying; she had the address because Olivia had asked her to forward her mail there.

He was shirtless and wearing only boxers when he answered the door. It was clear she'd awakened him when she rang the buzzer.

"I thought you might need lunch," she'd said, blushing as she held up the bag. She won't soon forget the look on his face—that sleepy, knowing smile—or the touch of his hand at the small of her back when he took the bag from her hands, thanked her, and invited her to join him.

* * *

AT THAT PARTICULAR MEMORY, Tess reaches into her bag below the table, pretending to search for her phone. She's certain her face will betray her.

Ari remains engrossed in his phone, or at least pretends to be, and Ines has opened a book. Only Esti keeps demanding Olivia's attention, climbing in and out of her lap, playing with her earrings.

Olivia pulls a notebook and box of crayons out of her bag. "Look what I still have! Draw me a picture, munchkin. Draw me a picture of the pretty new place where I work."

Esti slides obediently off her chair and situates herself on the floor below their table, spreading the crayons in a row. It hadn't even occurred to her, Tess realizes, to bring something to occupy Esti. With her older children, she would have never arrived so unprepared.

She blows on her tea, even though it's no longer hot. "Silvio says this virus is getting worse," she says. "He says it's showing up a lot in Italy, especially in the north." She coughs involuntarily, then gulps a sip of tea.

Olivia is staring at her now, saying nothing for what feels, to Tess, like a very long time. At last she shrugs. "I haven't talked to Charlie since he left," she says. "Do you think he might have had it or something?"

Tess scoots her chair back suddenly and scolds Esti for sitting on the dirty lobby floor. Even though she's been down there for a while by now.

· · ·

THE PLAN WAS FOR TESS to begin a new project. A new life really. She would research and write about two major art collectors of the twentieth century: Albert Barnes and

Calouste Gulbenkian. Gulbenkian was an Armenian businessman who had brokered a deal giving the British access to the Al-Jazeera oil fields in Iraq—and securing himself a five-percent share in the international oil industry that grew out of that deal. Snubbed by both the British and the French later in his life, he'd left the impressive collection he'd compiled in Paris to a museum bearing his name in Lisbon, his adopted home.

It was a beautiful museum, small and welcoming—as different from both versions of the Barnes Collection as it was possible to be. Soon after arriving in Lisbon, Tess had begun spending her days off there. More often than not she ended up in the café, sipping a coffee and watching parents with their children in the garden that was visible from the café's back window. Eventually she'd started taking Amalia there, on days when Rafa had soccer practice after school.

Amalia's favorites were the sixteenth-century tapestries, displayed in the darkened galleries housing the main collection's decorative arts. And always, before closing time, they'd stop to admire a nineteenth-century sculpture in marble that Amalia adored, *Winged Siren Seizing an Adolescent*, by Denys Puech. It seemed to make some people uncomfortable, Tess often noticed (the guards more than anyone), seeing this disabled girl's rapt fascination with the naked woman/bird/fish siren clutching an adolescent boy by his naked thigh. He doesn't exactly look unhappy about it, that seized naked boy, as the siren rests her head against his taut belly, his thigh held between her breasts.

Something about this work moved Amalia deeply. She loved Greek mythology; she often listened to an audio recording of a man's sensuous voice, reading Greek myths in Portuguese, to soothe her into sleep at night. Tess listened too, dozing in the big, comfy chair in the corner of Amalia's room, the same chair Silvio had sat in every night, reaching over to stroke his daughter's hair as he waited for her to fall asleep. From time to time, she caught references to Artemis and Persephone, Orpheus and Odysseus, oddly accented to her ear and also beautiful, arriving like a dream; her Portuguese was just short of rudimentary at that point. Not long after she arrived, Tess asked her mother to send her childhood copy of *D'Aulaires' Book of Greek Myths*, so she could share the illustrations with Amalia.

But Tess knew it was more than the myths that drew Amalia to Puech's sculpture. Tess had been a lonely girl with a handsome older brother herself; she'd watched his friends' easy physical grace—throwing a football, wrestling in the backyard—in the same way Amalia watched Rafa and his friends playing soccer. Shyly, hungrily, longing for that freedom, and for something else too, something she was just beginning to imagine.

So Tess ignored the museum guards' apparent discomfort, their impatience as they glanced repeatedly at their watches, clearing their throats and muttering about closing time. That sculpture belonged to Amalia as much as it belonged to anyone else; it was hers to stare at, to wonder about and long for, no matter how young, or physically limited, she was.

That's what Albert Barnes would have said, surely. Perhaps Calouste Gulbenkian too.

After their visits to the Gulbenkian, Tess would be buzzing with life—thirsty, famished, all her senses on high alert. The feeling returned, to some degree, years later, after trips to the museum with Ari and Ines. Once they started school she would, she thought, find some way to capture the experience of viewing the eclectic works in Gulbenkian's collection—the tapestries, the sculptures, the Chinese porcelains, the European paintings, the Lalique jewels and glass works—everything as rich and varied and idiosyncratic, in her estimation, as the collection of Albert Barnes. At least this was her hypothesis. One that remained untested now, more than ten years later, though not for lack of trying.

She'd gone dutifully to the Gulbenkian library—another place where her wealthy and well-connected husband could make arrangements—nearly every day for several months when Ines began grade one. She'd read books and articles, then gone back to stare at works in the museum, the tapestries, *Winged Siren Seizing an Adolescent*, all of it. She ended her days in the café, once again watching the parents with young children as they chased the ducks outside the cafe window.

If Modigliani had painted her, the title might have been *Redheaded woman with (empty) notebook*. Or, *Redheaded woman drinking coffee and watching younger women with their children*.

Once, on a whim, she sent an email to Les, who, she'd discovered online, was still teaching art history classes at the college she'd attended. Yes, of course he remembered her, he said in his quick reply, and after answering his polite questions about her, she wrote a sentence or two about the project she was trying and failing to begin. A comparison of the collections, and the shared experience of being outsiders, of Albert Barnes and Calouste Gulbenkian.

For a week she heard nothing from him. Then, when he finally answered, all he said was, "I'm sorry, but I just don't see it. Albert Barnes has nothing in common with an Armenian oil baron who hoarded expensive things that people already considered treasures in his Paris mansion."

Did Les actually know that about Gulbenkian, Tess wondered? Or had he just read the Wikipedia article? Most

Americans, in her experience, had no idea who Gulbenkian was, though of course most Americans also had no idea who Albert Barnes was. Les had probably just searched online for the first thing that came up about Gulbenkian. That way he could make the comparison he needed to make, conveniently overlooking the fact that Barnes was also an outrageously wealthy man by the time he started collecting art. Instead of oil, his wealth had come from promoting a partner chemist's formula for Argyrol, an antiseptic silver compound.

No matter really, Tess told herself. It wasn't Les who was blocking her from making any kind of progress. Probably he'd just helped her recognize the pointlessness of even trying. In the end she'd turned out to be what she'd always known she was, really: a charlatan. A bored wife and mother with zero academic credentials, spending more time in the museum café than in the library or among the collections. Not all that different, really, from the twenty-two-year-old nurse who'd sat in that same café with a notebook, watching parents with their children and thinking she would probably be better at that.

Even Silvio had seemed baffled. Not by her interest in Gulbenkian, not by her idea for a project on Gulbenkian and Barnes. By her inability to just *do* the thing—do the research, write the article. Just get on with it. When she told him about Les's response (pretending to laugh at it, pretending to find it funny), he'd simply stared at her for a moment, then said "And *who* is this man again?"

He was packing for a meeting in Brussels, and he was late. He didn't have time for another conversation about her project.

"You don't *have* to do any of that, you know," he'd said as he zipped his bag and rushed to meet his driver. He'd swept his arm in a wide arc as he said it, taking in their lavish bedroom, the giant apartment. As if to draw her attention to all she already had. As if to say, what *would* be the point, really?

So she'd gotten pregnant, with Esti. And after Esti's birth, she'd plunged into a dark and unfamiliar depression, unlike anything she'd experienced with her first two children.

Olivia was to be the solution. And she was, in many ways, for the year and a half year she was with them. Now Tess is stronger, clearer, ready to care for her children again, though anxious about that too, considering the fact that these days she is frequently lost in completely inappropriate daydreams and fantasies. So much so that she may have even exposed herself to a deadly virus.

A crowd has gathered in the plaza outside the building; street performers of some kind, maybe break dancers, have appeared there. Ines sees them first, and she asks if they can go outside to watch.

Olivia answers a text, then starts to tidy their table. "You all go ahead," she says. "I'm going out with some friends from work now. They'll be down soon." So they all say their goodbyes, and Olivia promises to visit the children soon.

Outside, the sky is clearing. It's turned into a lovely Friday evening, and clusters of tourists are stepping off trams and out of taxis and Ubers. No one on this plaza seems concerned about a virus, and each of Tess's children is, for the moment, happily occupied with watching the acrobatic dancers in front of them.

Of course, Tess knows how things will turn out. It's the way they always turn out for her, since meeting and falling in love with Silvio.

She'll ask him to arrange testing for the virus for her and all of the children, just to be safe. Olivia too, if she's willing.

All of them had been with Charlie after all, when he came to the apartment a week ago.

Olivia's new life, maybe including Charlie and surely other men, will go on, unknown and unrecognizable to Tess. A thing apart. The beginning of something so different, so removed, from Tess's own early years in Lisbon.

Tess's children will grow up and away from her—even demanding little Esti. Even Amalia hardly has time for Tess and Silvio now, caught up in her own friendships and romantic entanglements in the place where she's lived since she turned eighteen.

Had Tess heard Charlie coughing in the bathroom on Monday, after they ate lunch together? Or had she only felt that it would be fitting if he *was* coughing, if he was sick, and if she grew sick as well. That there would be a kind of logic, or justice, or something in that.

Even though she hadn't slept with him. Even though all they'd done was talk, and laugh, and enjoy the lavish lunch she'd brought together. Would he have slept with her, if she'd been forward enough to ask? She has no idea. How was a MILF to know?

Before she left, Charlie pulled her to him and kissed her in the apartment's open doorway. It was a full kiss, a luxuriant one, mouth-on-mouth. When it ended he held his forehead next to hers briefly, then smiled as he stepped away and closed the door. In the end, it would probably have been called a "chaste kiss" in a novel, Tess decided. Or worse (her fear): a sympathy kiss. Whatever kind of kiss it was, it was definitely enough to spread a toxic virus, if indeed he had it. Her head swirls with the embarrassment and the fear that have dogged her since Monday. Yet at the same time there's no denying this fact: She also wonders if and when she might see him again. Unlikely, she knows, even though Charlie had shared his number and invited her to call him if she's ever in Venice.

It's unlikely for lots of reasons. She and Silvio had gone to Venice some years ago, for their anniversary, and she'd mostly hated it. All those tourists, all those gondoliers playing recorded music, all that water. And the art—all of it, from the Bellinis to the Titians and Tintorettos to the eclectic collection of that other twentieth-century art fiend Peggy Guggenheim—had somehow left her cold.

Also, it sounds like no one will be traveling to Italy any time soon.

All her children are happy for the moment. Tess pretends to enjoy the performers along with them, though watching their pleasure now can't begin to compare to those days with Amalia, at the Gulbenkian. When she turns to look back at the building behind them, she sees Olivia and her friends emerging from the revolving door, talking and laughing as they walk in the direction of the Avenida da Liberdade. There are two young men and two young women, plus Olivia.

The other women, Tess notices, are wearing dresses that are just like Olivia's—low-cut, form-fitting, beautiful and youthful and free. But still Olivia stands apart in her dress, Tess's dress, which is red, and vivid, and memorable.

Esti tugs at her sleeve, then her hand. The dancers have finished, and the crowd is dispersing. Her children want to leave. But Tess ignores them, still watching Olivia and her friends. She watches them until the throng of people surrounds them, and the bright flame of her old dress disappears.

PHILADELPHIA,
APRIL
2020

Disembarkation Sickness

I'VE BEEN AWAKE SINCE DAWN, sitting at the French doors in my kitchen and watching the late April light creep across my back garden. Which needs pruning. Which needs cleared beds and plans for planting. Which needs the pots brought from the shed, the pool cover cleared of brush.

But now it's close to 10:00 A.M., and still Tom isn't here. He didn't come last week either. He doesn't pick up when I try to call; nothing new there. I worry, though, that I may have driven him away by asking, as I did when I saw him last, if he would bring me something for the pain one more time.

It's bad again this morning, the worst it's been maybe, and the nausea is kicking in now as well. At ten in the morning I am considering a drink, pondering which might be easier on my sensitive stomach: whiskey or vodka.

Tom slanted his eyes at me when I asked. As Tom knows, everything I could possibly want or need is at my fingertips—the means to bring my son home, surgery, the best pain medicines available, even, perhaps, "a new, and also old, adventure," in the words of my son's father. At the moment, however, we are in the midst of a plague. And I would like Tom to come as requested. I would like him to bring me a pill to take, something to rid me of this sickness, this *mal de débarquement*, as I've begun calling it in my mind. So that I might dig my hands into the cold spring earth, into dirt that's barely thawed from winter. Every plant I move, every seed I plant, a new beginning. A break with the past, a washing away of the stain of this dreadful moment. Something new, something set apart—something climbing toward a different sun.

I've noticed that when the pain is vanquished, interestingly, the nausea disappears as well. The nausea reminds me of seasickness, that roiling malaise that seems so out of keeping with the vast beauty that surrounds you on a boat. But besides seasickness, there is something else: disembarkation sickness, or *mal de débarquement*. You feel like you're still on the boat, rocking and swaying (also confused, anxious, maybe very tired), even though you've been on solid ground for a long time. It's most common in middle-aged women, which must mean something. It may be linked with migraines.

There's no name, however, for this particular thing I'm experiencing, this malady that seems to have worsened since I heard from Michael, my son's father. Nausea, yes, but mostly I'm experiencing exhaustion, and resistance. Resistance to boarding that old, vaguely familiar boat at all, and fatigue at the very thought. Fatigue with boats, fatigue with romance and new adventures. Who needs any of that really, at my age? Even my son Charlie seems tired of it all now. And he's a strapping American male who's not yet thirty.

I suppose I'm to blame for the fact that Charlie's only apparent aspiration is to read poetry. To be fair, he also writes some things of his own occasionally. What he writes and performs is poetry of a sort, I suppose—more like rap or hip-hop I think, though I'm not sure how these differ from each other or from poetry or from "spoken word," as Charlie sometimes calls what he does. My ignorance doesn't seem to bother him. My son stopped expecting me to understand him or his world at around age ten.

I too was an avid reader, at least as a child. My mother didn't have time to read much herself, but she recognized reading as my ticket out of the world where I was born to a failed farmer and his defeated wife. I've spent more than half my life keeping that piece of my past to myself.

Each year at Christmas and my birthday my mother bought me new books. I've kept a handful of them. In the earliest Golden books my name is written on the inside cover in my mother's blocky print; in *Heidi* and *The Black Stallion* my name, Nina Rae Dietrich, appears in my own studied cursive, the pencil's lead faint to begin with and fading further with the passage of time.

Now I hold a book, any book, and it feels heavy in my hands. Even the flimsiest paperback. My eyes glaze with sleep. I do very little reading these days, even though I'm a donor and a volunteer at the Philadelphia Free Library, and my sense is that I'm not alone. What can it mean in a world like this, and at a time like this, that my son Charlie wants to be a poet? Which means he spends most of his time in bars, occasionally performing but mostly drinking and getting into fights. Is this what it means to be a poet now? And if so, how does the story of a poet's life *end*?

No believable story ends well. None but the most insipid ones do, and maybe that's why so few of us read anymore. In truth I'd rather be in the garden or looking at seed catalogs when it's too cold to work out there. Even with my tender back, the stabs of pain along my hips and legs, my stiff and aching shoulders and arms. Yoga and swimming have helped, and so when I'm not in my garden that's mostly what I do, or what I've done until now. I've realized recently that I prefer these things—yoga, swimming, gardening or dreaming about gardens—to traveling to the other side of the world to sun myself on one of Geoffrey's boats.

Geoffrey is, I suppose, my boyfriend, and from all outward indicators he is a good one. He's five years younger than I am, funny, attractive, sexually solicitous, capable of being in the same room as my son. Easy all around really. Except for the boats. And the fact that he drinks quite a lot, and that I'm always all too happy, relieved actually, to join him.

Michael, Charlie's father, recently wrote to me on one of my social media accounts, and against my better judgment I responded. We've had a little back-and-forth message exchange going since the lockdown began. Playful, goading, flirtatious—oddly so, considering our circumstances.

We're behaving as if that particular wave hadn't passed quite a while ago. Aren't we all long finished with those rounds of trial and error—with finding someone you loved in the past online and hoping for a flicker of something there still? Instead, we've been driven deeper into privacy, farther from the possibility of fresh starts. A pandemic will do that to you, I guess. But apparently not to Michael; he thinks he has a solution to viruses, and to riots too.

But then, Michael was always late to the party. "And often the first to leave." That's how he described himself on the first night I went to his apartment with him. Why stay, if no one had anything to smoke or quaff or ingest that was as good as any number of things he had waiting back at his place? And people rarely did.

This was at Penn State, in the nineties. Not exactly the kind of place you'd imagine the heir to a giant pharmaceutical fortune to land, but Michael's grades were mediocre, and those were days of higher principles on the part of his family members, at least. Actually, it probably had nothing to do with principles; they hadn't tried to buy Michael a spot at a better school because why bother? None of them was a product of the Ivy League, but that hadn't stopped them from inheriting company shares and lucrative jobs at a business that got its start in Michael's great-grandfather's kitchen on the north side of Chicago—the kitchen where Maxwell Milford, a dabbler in chemicals, began making something called "therapeutic colloidal medicinals" in the 1920s.

I might have tried to do that for Charlie, to be honest, had he let me. Throw some of the family money at a place like Swarthmore or Haverford maybe. But my son chose a no-name school west of the city, where he thought he might play basketball, and I let him go there, prep school diploma be damned. I've never managed my son's life well, people might say. Have said. His father has been a particularly pointed— if sporadic and more frequently absent or bored or both— critic of my parenting.

"We could embark on a new, and also old, adventure," Michael began the message on my phone a month ago. It was early in the morning, the sun beginning to brighten the leaves of the oakleaf hydrangea outside my window. I was in the kitchen, waiting to greet Tom with our usual thermos of coffee and jug of water. Still hoping he'd show up for one of our regular workdays, though I hadn't heard from him since he came the week before.

I'd long ago turned off notifications on my phone, so by the time I noticed the message that morning, it had been there for several days. My contact with Charlie's father has generally been via email, occasionally a rushed call. Why, I wondered, was he messaging me on Facebook? Yet when I read the message, Michael's way of speaking—casual and glib, projecting self-awareness but not actually achieving it—was immediately familiar. Who else would use a phrase like "embark on an adventure" for, presumably, another stab at a sexual relationship? Though he hasn't spoken to me in that particular way for nearly twenty years.

I'll admit there was a quiver of something inside me when I read his message, pathetic as that is. Suddenly I was a naïve college sophomore again, noticed by this pretty rich boy, this stoner junior, who—unlike so many other college guys who'd pursued me—was as tall as I was. And also very attractive, his teeth straight and white, his lips soft and lush, blond curls tumbling over the collar of his flannel shirt. That's who I remembered as I read his message, which appeared out of the blue after five years with essentially no contact between us. That Michael. The Penn State one, the tall, languorous, and lovely one I'd fallen for long ago. Not the one I'd known for the thirty years since we were college students.

The voice of that long-ago Michael had been seductive, husky with lust—so unlike the terse and business-like voice of the man with whom I've discussed our son's health and athletic and educational expenses, and through the years, his occasional need for bail. That more recent Michael had been a spectral presence, consulting on the phone or via email as needed while he and his second wife raised their two children in northern California. On the day the younger child from that marriage left for college, Michael had initiated divorce proceedings. Two months after that, his message arrived on my phone.

He still looked good in his profile photo, though of course older, fuller in the jaw as happens with men. Straight men with money don't have to worry about such things. Whereas

I've spent the last ten years avoiding fats and carbs and exercising daily, getting frequent facials and occasional jabs of Botox. Had I *not* done these things, I'm certain Michael's message would not have suddenly appeared on my screen.

Actually, I might embark on any number of adventures in the years ahead; I have options, too many of them probably. Probably that's my problem. Michael's offering one, and it has a certain appeal but also certain liabilities. Boredom being one. I've dated so many wealthy men by now, men with boats and golf course tans and third homes in places like Key West and Costa Rica, and there has been an undeniable sameness in my experiences with these men, no matter where they came from or how they acquired their wealth.

Yes, Michael has photos of his paintings on his page, and news about start-up arts organizations that he's supporting as a founding board member. But I know, beyond a doubt, that by a third or fourth week of being together, he'd mostly be talking about money. Schemes for sheltering it, more real estate to buy with it, new market ventures, the S&P 500 and crypto currencies and NFTs and blah, blah, blah. And his eyes, as he speaks, would be roving, scanning the horizon for younger flesh. The tedious, predictable *sameness* of it all.

Once, when I complained to Liliane about the conversational limitations of the men I seemed to keep meeting and dating, she said "Well, you don't have to *listen* to them, do you? You're beautiful, you're desirable, you will be for years—you can use this to your advantage. When they talk just tune them out. Let your mind travel elsewhere. Think about Charlie, think about the book you're reading or the movie you just saw, something like that. That's what I would do."

"Not that this is a problem I've experienced," she added, taking a long drag on her Pall Mall. It amazes me, still, that Liliane smoked the same dreadful cigarettes that my mother smoked for years. And then died as my mother apparently had as well: painfully, despite a steady morphine drip, both of them with lungs shot through with cancer.

We were sitting by Liliane's pool that day, and it was hot. I was sweating in the noon heat, wearing a bikini and working on my tan before leaving for a month on the boat of an import/export guy from Chile, someone I'd met at a private donors' event at the library. Liliane was in one of the spacious, gauzy dresses she wore throughout the summer, fanning herself languidly though she didn't appear to be hot. Liliane never seemed to notice the heat, or the cold. Something about her ample body seemed to protect her from both.

"I certainly didn't have what you have," she continued that day, and it wasn't the first time I'd heard this, nor would it be the last. "No Scandinavian bone structure. No growing the family fortune that way."

Liliane had a limp from a bout of polio when she was a child, and a lazy eye. Which was surprising really, in the one living child of Maxwell Milford, founder of the MilCor pharmaceutical and household goods conglomerate. Liliane could easily have had both remedied surgically. But for Liliane it seemed to be a lifelong source of pride not to have done so. A kind of badge of honor.

Instead of an heiress and philanthropist, Liliane had wished to be a poet. Unfortunately, she was apparently not a good one, so heiress and philanthropist it had to be. I'm not the only person who recognizes that Liliane bequeathed a generous portion of her family's fortune to an obscure library and magazine, in a city she'd never visited, as a way of telling the remaining members of the extended Milford tribe to fuck themselves.

And good for her. All the Milfords treated her horribly. But Michael, her grand-nephew, was an exception of sorts. He was kind, on the rare occasions he saw Liliane—on holidays when he was a student, and then on random and unannounced visits when he blew through Philadelphia to see his son. He believes that's why she also provided nicely for Charlie in her will. It's in keeping with Michael's particular brand of rich man's narcissism to have failed to notice that Liliane cared deeply about Charlie because she loved me. Just as I loved her.

Despite the fact that she offered endless, mostly unsolicited, advice. That she controlled most aspects of my life for twenty-five years. That she convinced me, early on, that I was better off with her and well apart from my poor family, still struggling along on a blighted piece of land in a desolate, dying coal region. That she urged me, in no uncertain terms, to end my relationship with Silvio, the only man since Michael who I thought I could truly love.

I did as she wished. And that was that.

. . .

I WAS PREGNANT when I came to live with Liliane. There would be no abortion, she announced when Michael and I arrived at her home during my sophomore year at Penn State, and no putting a Milford child up for adoption. I would have the child and live with her, she decreed, caring for my child in her home in Lower Merion with her resources at my disposal. And then, as she grew older, I would oversee *her* care, and Michael would oversee those resources.

"And of course Michael will marry her, after graduation," said Robert, Liliane's brother and Michael's grandfather, withering from liver disease at the age of seventy. For the inheritors of a fortune originating with therapeutic medicinal colloidals the Milfords were a magnificently unhealthy and damaged lot. Michael's father was dead from cancer by age forty-two; his mother drove her car into a tree the day she was released from rehab, when Michael was eighteen. Robert, his grandfather, would die six months after that meeting in Liliane's home, shortly before his great grandson Charlie was born.

Liliane said nothing that day in her lavish parlor, winking in our direction. Only after Robert had hobbled out her front door did she return to the subject of marriage.

"I wouldn't allow you to marry even if you wanted to," she said. "You're both far too young, and obviously immature. Too young and immature to raise a child as well, which is why that needs to happen here, with the help I'll hire."

I remember looking around then, taking in my surroundings for the first time. The rug beneath our feet, which I'd been trained to call an oriental rug, was vast and thick, a swirl of intricately woven threads in deep purples and reds. All the furniture was made of supple leather and burnished oak—Liliane's Cavalier King Charles spaniels were forbidden in this, the main parlor—and there were real paintings, created by artists I'd actually heard of, on the wall.

When we left Liliane's home that day Michael practically skipped to his car, a cobalt blue Maserati that he'd parked behind his grandfather's chauffeured BMW. He was off the hook completely, and he was giddy with relief. We drove back to State College in silence. Michael tried, a few times, to make light conversation before he gave up and turned up the music, assuming I was angry.

I was and I wasn't. What I felt was a mixture of relief and shame. Shame not at being the fallen woman, the pregnant girl who would have to quit school, but at something I'd actually realized a month before, on the day Michael broke up with me—before I knew I was pregnant. Which was that Michael was ashamed of me. Ashamed and, probably, embarrassed to have bound himself in any way to someone like me.

I had met Michael at an off-campus party on a brisk autumn night. Back at his apartment that first night we were awkward lovers—our long limbs somehow getting in the way, giggling and bumbling and too drunk to mind. I'd been with only one boy before that, if you could call it being with him; I hadn't especially wanted to have sex with that boy, but I was also stone-cold sober, and I hadn't explicitly said no, and in those days that amounted to a yes in pretty much everyone's book.

But Michael was different. He was beautiful and sweetly tender. I wanted him to show me things, to teach me about sex. I hadn't expected him to be shy.

We got better at it after that, and soon we were leaving parties, often ones in Michael's own living room, early. We couldn't wait to leap at one another like two eager horses, all tensed muscles and long, twining legs, on his futon mattress on the floor. Afterwards we listened to R.E.M. and read poetry, sprawled naked under the beam of a single lamp. Nothing terribly surprising, no one not on the syllabus from one of our classes (both of us were English majors)—e.e. cummings, Sylvia Plath, Wallace Stevens. We read those poems aloud and pretended to understand them. Michael liked "Thirteen Ways of Looking at a Blackbird," but my favorite Wallace Stevens poem was "The Motive for Metaphor," which at certain moments I can still recite from memory. *You like it under the trees in autumn, because everything is half dead* . . . I found myself reciting it just yesterday, as I pruned my woodland asters and slowly scooted two potted hibiscus plants outdoors. *In the same way you were happy in spring, with the half colors of quarter things.* . . .

I was naïve to imagine my relationship with Michael going on like that forever, but who wouldn't have been at nineteen? The end arrived sooner than even Michael expected, I think, and it was a terrible blow to me. The beginning of that end came in March, at the start of a wintry spring break week, when we were traveling north with several of Michael's friends, to ski. We'd left late, and the roads had quickly grown hazardous. We'd been drinking—Michael, who was driving, more than any of us—and I was anxious. So I said we could stop to spend the night at my parents' house, which was only fifteen miles off the turnpike.

That night, for the first time, I saw my childhood home through the eyes of someone like Michael. The vinyl siding on the tract home that had long ago replaced the farmhouse. The rutted, empty fields, the rusted mowers and plows and cars poking out of the blanketing snow. The bedroom to which one of my two older brothers had returned—estranged from the wife he said had tried to kill him—and where he now snored raucously, sleeping off whatever meth-fueled adventure he'd last returned from. My mother's hacking cough from behind her closed bedroom door. The stained recliner where my father had spent his last days, before dying from diabetes-related complications when I was in tenth grade.

I watched Michael as he listened to these noises and looked around, trying to take it all in. And in that moment I understood that this world—my world—simply could not be absorbed by someone like him. For the rest of the week, at a lodge in Vermont, he was tender with me. Pitying me, I suspected, and clearly on the cusp of breaking up with me. As inexperienced as I was, I'm not sure how I knew this. But I did.

So I did not use my diaphragm for the entire week (though I claimed, later, to have forgotten it only once, when we were especially drunk). Clearly the wrong time to forget it, I said to Michael a month later, by phone. The night we returned from Vermont he'd asked me to move my things out of his room. And I hadn't seen him since.

Since falling for Michael, I had begun to picture a very different future for myself, a way out of the world I'd grown up in. Once I realized he would not be my rescuer after all, at least not in the way I'd imagined, I saw no reason to try to prevent a pregnancy, or to take any other meaningful steps or precautions. When I learned I was pregnant I turned every decision about my future over to Michael. *Here*, I suppose I was saying to him. *You're rich. Deal with this.*

At the end of that spring semester I finished my final papers and exams, at Liliane's insistence. Occasionally I caught glimpses of Michael, driving in his car or walking out of one of the classroom buildings. We waved like casual friends. After my last exam he drove me to Liliane's house on the Main Line, his car's tiny trunk filled with the contents of my dorm room—the old and torn quilt my grandmother had made, a box of books, and two suitcases packed with t-shirts and shorts and jeans that were growing tight.

What else could I have done? I was pregnant, and I could not, or I *would* not, go home to my mother's house. By then I couldn't bear the thought of returning there in any state. The only way out of the situation, it seemed to me, was to carry through with what Liliane had proposed: to live with her and give birth to my child and see what would happen after that.

When Liliane insisted that I write to my mother to explain my situation, I did so. Liliane edited my letter, softening it, making me promise to visit with the baby in the spring. And in May, I did visit my mother one last time. On Mother's Day, with five-month-old Charlie in tow.

"He looks nothing like you," my mother said that day, scowling at Charlie, or me, or both of us—I wasn't sure—as I sat in a lawn chair behind the house, nursing him.

She was right, I realized, startled. It hadn't even occurred to me that my child might look like me. Of course he would look like Michael, and he did. In a certain way I didn't even think of him as mine. He was, and remains, blond and blue-eyed, with his father's lithe frame and winning smile. No hint of my tawny hair or green eyes, the spray of freckles across my nose. He's a virtual twin of the Michael I first knew.

For the next twenty-plus years, until Liliane's death, I did as she told me. Now that she's gone, the lavish Milford home occupied by some distant cousin, my own comfortable home purchased for Charlie and me long ago, and my son well provided for, I am not sure what to do. And so I consider embarking on Michael's proposed adventure, ridiculous as it seems.

The adventure Michael is offering does not involve a boat, or water. In fact, it involves a landlocked farm west of Philadelphia, near the crumbling city of Reading. Someone tried, and failed, to create a winery on that farm. But according to Michael that person didn't really know what he was doing.

"Not because you can't grow grapes there. You can grow beautiful grapes there. I've seen photos; that part was going fine. This guy just lacked basic business acumen, and he didn't have enough capital to launch a functioning winery."

Of course, Michael has the capital. So maybe two of the three—the grapes, the capital—are enough. Because there's still no business acumen in the plan he has in mind. He thinks Charlie can manage this thing.

"He was an English major," I typed in response. "Like you."

"I know that. And I also know he's smart, and a good communicator. A poet for God's sake! We're talking about marketing here. The poetry of wine."

That was such a ridiculous thing to say, and so typical of Michael. I said nothing in reply but filed it away to laugh about later, with Charlie. Then I thought about Min, and her big extended family, most of whom live in Reading. Charlie would like the location at least, I thought but didn't type.

Apparently, Michael thinks it makes more sense to buy a failing winery in Pennsylvania than to invest in one where he's lived for the past twenty years: Sonoma County. He has his reasons for choosing a rural backwater in Pennsylvania, he says. Saner taxes, to start with. Far from western droughts and fires. A pliable immigrant work force. Reasonable proximity to Philadelphia and New York, but enough distance to avoid riots and viral outbreaks. All those Silicon Valley preppers with their underground bunkers have the wrong idea, he says. Better to build your bunker in the heart of Pennsylvania Dutch country.

I also assume he prefers the thought of being on the other side of the country from wife number two. He moved to California twenty years ago, after all, in flight from wife number one, who lives in New York.

Before Michael moved to California, we'd flirted briefly with the idea of being together, the three of us, as a family. Michael was spending time at Liliane's, and at my house, playing basketball with Charlie, who was ten—maybe his most likeable age. He was also connecting with old friends from high school and college and "weighing his options," he said, "figuring out next steps." He'd tried working for a hedge fund in New York but found it boring. Maybe it was time to settle in and take on a role at MilCor.

I remember he was in sweaty tennis whites from a morning game at Liliane's club, flopped thoughtlessly on her leather sofa as if he was still a college student, when he shared these thoughts with Liliane and me. He was still handsome, maybe even more so at that point; he'd gained just enough weight to look substantial instead of gangly. His hair, now a sophisticated gray-blond, was expensively trimmed, his mouth still lush and inviting. Part of me wanted to kiss it; another felt exhausted at the thought. What "role," exactly, did he imagine was waiting for him at MilCor?

Liliane cocked an eyebrow at me, as if reading my mind. "You'll have to speak to one of your cousins about that, I'm afraid," she said. "As you know, my dealings are only with the foundation. They've more or less banished me from the business side of things. Not that I've objected."

In the end he never called his cousins. Later that day he dug an old tuxedo out of one of Liliane's closets, and that night he joined us at a benefit for the Philadelphia Orchestra at the brand new Kimmel Center. We hardly saw him once we got there. Wife number two was there that night as well, tending bar.

Once again I was left alone to raise our son, with more than adequate resources, of course. I still seem to be raising him, or trying to.

There are other ways to be an adult male, I've said to Charlie. Look at Geoffrey, who works for his family business and travels the world and tends lovingly to his four boats and—in Charlie's own words—"isn't a complete asshole."

Also, look at what you have at your disposal. A home and a likely job in Philadelphia, or, if you'd prefer, in Chicago, in the poetry wing of a private library that your family has funded for perpetuity. That library is indebted to us, as is the magazine they publish. Or, well, to the family. Which, now, basically means you and me.

But Charlie hates such suggestions. They're connected with his father, for one thing. For another, work at the library would be an act of "brazen nepotism"—his term. That'll be the case with pretty much any paid work you might end up doing, I've often thought but refrained from saying to him. So is the endless and aimless traveling you were doing until a global pandemic stanched your post-college flood of restlessness. All made possible by your father's family's money and the connections that go along with that. Welcome to the world you were born into, Charlie.

For now, all I want is for him to come home. To get out of Venice, to be far away from Italy, where the virus has been raging for weeks. But now, of all times, he seems to have found a purpose: salvaging a dead man's bookstore and helping that man's wife and children flee the city. There in the brutal heart of a terrifyingly contagious, and deadly, disease.

Come back, I need to tell him. Come home to a farm near Min's mother. Come compose the poetry of wine. Rescue all of us—Min's mother, Tom, me. And in the process, maybe, win back your one true love.

• • •

MIN IS DETERMINED and hardworking and devoted to her family, especially her mother. I know more about her than Charlie has ever realized. We used to talk when she was first out of college and new to her job as an ER nurse. Then a year ago, when the hospital where she worked was sold, Min and two hundred other nurses were laid off. I worried about her. For a moment. She's an excellent nurse (I know this because Tom has told me), and within a month she'd been hired at the Philadelphia V.A. Hospital, in acute care.

For a while, Min was commuting from her mother's apartment in Reading. She worried about bringing the virus home, so I offered her a room in my house. Which was not as virtuous as it might sound. This place is cavernous, and for the month she lived here, until she moved in with another nurse in West Philadelphia, I hardly saw Min. The only sign she was even here was the sound of her shitty car, a rusted old Toyota that growled to life when she left at 7:00 A.M., then rumbled back into the driveway twelve or more hours later. If she ate anything, I never saw any sign of it. I think she was probably too tired to eat. *Thanks*, she'd text back when I told her about something I'd left in the refrigerator, *but I think I'm just gonna shower and go to bed.*

For years, after college, she and Charlie were on and off, hot and cold. There were more break-ups than I could count. I always knew it had happened again when Charlie showed up at the house, burrowing in his room or spending hours shooting baskets at the hoop behind the house. I still can't bring myself to take that thing down, though Tom has offered more than once to remove it. He seems to have a blinkered view of Charlie, though that hasn't come from me. Definitely from Min.

Things are different now though. Now my son and his sometime girlfriend are nearly thirty. Min has no time for Charlie. And Charlie spends his days boxing up and shipping online orders from the shuttered bookstore where he was working when the owner died of the virus. In a weak moment I wired him money to buy the store's contents from the owner's wife. Most of my moments with my son seem to be weak ones.

Somehow Charlie has procured a special visa connected with this venture. Perhaps Geoffrey helped him with that too, just as he arranged for his comfortable room in some sort of art collective where Charlie was staying until recently, when the bookstore owner's wife and children moved somewhere to the north, and Charlie took over their apartment. I can't picture any part of my son's life at this point; I've stopped trying.

"So are you planning to stay in Italy indefinitely?" I asked when I sent him the money. "Are you planning to be a bookstore owner?" Ridiculously impractical, now more than ever—but at least it would be *something*, I thought.

"No idea" was his answer, by text. "Taking things one day at a time right now."

Since hearing from Michael, I grow dizzy and nauseated at the thought of answering him, and yet I find myself wondering. Might a winery near Reading bring Charlie home?

Might it even cure my pain? The pain that doctors repeatedly suggest I must be imagining, or at least magnifying. Blowing it out of proportion, as women do. No doctor has actually said this to me directly, but they might as well have. One learns to read these people's bored, distracted, and patronizing countenances, as Liliane—who despised all doctors—used to say. Blood tests and X-rays and MRIs have revealed nothing but a mildly herniated disc. Probably I also have carpal tunnel syndrome, one doctor told me, before jabbing me with two cortisone shots and forgetting to tell me to call him in the morning.

Cortisone, by the way, can't hold a candle to the pills Tom brings me. Tom doesn't like to see people suffering, he says. He's a seventy-four-year-old Vietnam vet who's still wiry and strong. At certain moments—when his hair is longer, when a lit cigarette dangles from the corner of his mouth—he reminds me of Keith Richard. He rarely takes the pills he procures, now. Or so he tells me.

"I can bring you something that'll help," he told me last fall, the last time I tried to roll an overfull wheelbarrow on my own. "But it'd probably be easier if you just asked your doctor."

I wouldn't give the man the satisfaction, I told Tom that day. "He offered, believe me. You should have seen the smirk on his face. I suppose he thinks I'm making up the pain, just to get some kind of drug from him."

Tom nodded slowly. "They mostly think people are making it up," he said. "But at least he's willing to give you something anyway."

"Rich people and vets," he added, steering me toward a garden bench and taking over the wheelbarrow. "We're the ones they're happy to prescribe for."

• • •

THIS IS NOT SOMETHING I would have expected, but in the last five years I've grown completely enamored of gardening. I even completed a series of classes and earned a certificate in horticulture from a nearby university. Not the undergraduate degree Liliane always wanted me to complete, but at least it was something. It was gardening that saved me really, that lifted me out of the well of grief and aimlessness I fell into when Liliane died.

I wasn't her actual caretaker, not at the end, when she was essentially blind and unable to walk or control her bladder or bowels. For that we relied on a series of cheerful women with lilting Caribbean accents. But by the time she died, Liliane felt like the one person, besides my son, that I'd truly loved. I had lived with, or near, her for more than twenty-five years. She was my closest and dearest friend.

She'd also made every vital decision for me since I was twenty years old. Where, or to whom, would I turn for such guidance now?

Certainly not my own family. My mother died when Charlie was fifteen months old. I took him with me to her funeral, a small and sad affair in an old clapboard church at the edge of a dusty field. The only person I knew at that funeral was the older of my two brothers, who'd moved to West Virginia when I was in junior high school. He reported two things to me that day: that our other brother was in prison, and that there hadn't been a will. So, he said, the land and the house and what equipment was left all went to him, and he'd already sold them all. He hoped I understood.

I told him that I did. Then I drove home, with Charlie asleep in his car seat behind me. I am completely untethered, I thought, and I was still young enough, and perhaps still awash in enough nursing-induced hormones, to think that was a good thing. But years later, when Liliane died, being untethered felt different.

I felt alone. And after the funeral, back in my house, I *was* alone; Charlie had left for Min's home in Reading as soon as the service was over, and Michael spent the rest of the day meeting with lawyers before taking the redeye back to California.

As if to test the idea, I said it aloud into the silence of my house. *I am completely alone.* Then I shouted it, for good measure. My voice echoed as if I were in a mausoleum.

For nearly a year I left the house only to shop for groceries and liquor, and to swim at the club. But then a neighbor convinced me to enroll in that first horticulture class at the Barnes Arboretum, which featured the gardens of art collector Albert Barnes's wife Laura. Their empty mansion, and those gardens, were a ten-minute walk from my house, and as ridiculous as this seems to me now, I'd never once explored the grounds before I enrolled in that class. As soon as I did, I fell in love with Laura Leggett Barnes's fragrant lilacs in the spring, then the shaded, mossy green of her valley of ferns in summer.

"I have confidence in the laws of morals as of botany," said Ralph Waldo Emerson in a quote my first horticulture instructor included at the top of a handout on perennials. Emerson could count on his parsley, chestnuts, and acorns to return each year. Plants *are* something you can count on— more reliably, I would say, than morals. Or other people.

Geoffrey would probably say, "Why do women refuse to *trust* anyone?" He asked me that recently, out of the blue. As I'd said nothing about trust, or the lack thereof, and as he'd posed this question right after stepping outside to take a call, I assumed he wasn't referring to me.

Liliane hated gardening; she left that, like so many things, to other people. And Min has told me that if it were up to her, she would heave all her mother's tottering, flaking terra cotta pots—crowding her small apartment, filled with pepper plants and tomatoes and herbs and leggy, ancient geraniums—into the alley behind her building.

Two years ago, I poured potting soil into a giant glazed pot from Portugal, and when I lifted it to move it to the other side of the stone path that wends through the garden, something snapped. I sat down hard on the damp ground, breathless from the pain. It was the herniated disc. Daggers of pain traveling from my lower back down the sciatic nerve of my right leg. That was the beginning of something that's grown steadily worse. Now Tom lifts all the heavy pots and shovels most of the mulch.

Min recommended Tom, when I persuaded her to meet me for lunch one day and asked her about finding help. She raised an eyebrow at first, when I asked if she knew anyone I might hire. I know she assumed I was asking about a family member, one of her uncles or cousins, and I suppose she was right. Well, she *was* right. But Tom was someone she'd met at the hospital; he'd been a patient of hers.

Tom's reliable, until he isn't. His days are a mystery to me. He comes when he can, and not just for the money; he also comes because he loves digging in the soil and gently tending to plants. Sometimes he disappears for weeks and then I assume he's using, probably sleeping somewhere under a bridge in Kensington. Back before they closed his favorite hospital it was Min who saw him when he surfaced, at the ER.

Min is someone people tend to confide in; I know Tom has told her some things about his life. With me Tom is mostly silent. We work together in pleasant, quiet harmony, pausing now and then to drink some coffee and then, as the day heats up, for sips of cold water. I always offer Tom a sandwich at lunchtime, but it seems he is never hungry. Like Min he subsists, I think, on air.

At times I think my garden could be enough. A farm I'm less certain about.

What Michael is proposing—this idea of a winery and a reunited family—is preposterous. For too many reasons to list. I know this. I also know this will not happen, if it's left up to Michael. He is not a reliable person, at least where his son and his son's mother are concerned.

And yet, yesterday I made the ninety-minute drive west, to see this farm for myself. The sun was shining, and the place was deserted; I parked my car behind a big stone barn with a Pennsylvania Dutch hex sign and got out and walked around. Everything was perfectly tended, the neatly terraced fields of grape vines climbing a hill behind the fieldstone farmhouse, which was nestled in a valley formed by gently rolling hills. Crocuses and daffodils bloomed in corners of the wide lawn between the house and a patch of woods. The air smelled clean, like a fresh beginning. No reek of manure or fertilizer; it was entirely different from the hardscrabble rural world I'd known as a child. Also, there were no other people. Not a single other person wearing a mask.

Suddenly everything seemed to click into place. I peeked inside the barn and saw a vast emptiness; nothing in there but an old tractor, with sunlight pouring in from the loft above. We could put an apartment in that loft, I thought. We could hire Tom full-time and get him out of the unhealthy city.

And Charlie could move into the farmhouse and run the business. He'd be close to Min's family; he could win her back. We could build another apartment in the barn, for Min's mother. I could learn about growing grapes properly. And the gardens I could have at this place! Countless varieties of ferns in the shaded dell behind the farmhouse, verdant boxwoods lining the drive that curves back to the house from the highway. An herb garden the size of my pool back in Lower Merion.

For the span of the day, and my drive home, and the better part of last night, I somehow imagined that there in that quiet rural space—miles from the Philadelphia Main Line and a life I'd accepted without question for all these years—I could start again.

The big shaker of martinis I made for myself as soon as I got home kept the dream going for a while. Actually, the martinis magnified the dream. So much so that I got reckless with my phone. Not so reckless that I wrote to Michael, or even to Charlie. Instead, I wrote to Min.

I asked her what she thought of my ideas. Of Tom there in the barn, her mother there at the farm too, in her own safe space. A guest suite somewhere for me. Charlie in the big farmhouse—and maybe Min too. She could get out of Philadelphia hospitals for a while. She could wait out the run of this horrible virus.

I said it all, in a long, rambling, and obviously drunken text. I made myself read what I wrote when I woke up this morning, thankful it wasn't quite as bad as I'd feared. I sounded almost sane and sober by the end of my message, when I said I was eager to get to work in the garden in the morning and wondered if she'd heard anything from Tom.

But so far Min hasn't responded. And this morning, the pain is bad and getting worse.

• • •

"LET'S SEE IF WE CAN HOME IN on what's going on," said a pain specialist I saw in February, back when we were cavalierly walking into hospitals and medical offices, unmasked and blissfully unaware of what was coming. This specialist looked younger than my son.

He handed me an electronic tablet with the usual questions, culminating with the one I hate the most. Assign your pain a number. Rank it on a scale of 1 to 10.

I barked out a noise, something between a laugh and an exasperated cry, and tossed the tablet onto the examining table.

"I can't assign my pain a number," I said. "And I'm sick of being asked to do that."

He was surprisingly nonplussed—accustomed, maybe, to raging middle-aged women in search of relief.

"Okay, that's fine. Why don't you just try to tell me what you experience, then? How would you describe it? Try putting it into words."

I stared at him for a moment, trying to decide if he was mocking me. It was impossible to tell; I've never seen a blanker, younger, more innocuous face.

So I began. "It generally starts in my thighs," I said. "I know it's coming on when I feel spasms in my inner thighs. It moves quickly after that. My lower back freezes up; I can't move freely. I also find it difficult to breathe. It's like someone is sitting on my chest, threatening me with mortal injury if I breathe loudly enough to make a sound. When I try to stand and walk, my legs feel like they're radically different lengths. I can't move normally. I walk with something like a limp, only it's worse. I have to drag one leg behind me. Usually my right leg, sometimes my left. It varies. I don't know why. Before long, my feet grow numb, except when they start to cramp. And the joints in my arms—my shoulders and my elbows—register another kind of pain, an ache that stops my breath and makes me feel like I might throw up every time I try to lift something or raise an arm above my head. Walking is agony. Sitting or lying down is worse.

"Sometimes," I concluded, "it seems best if I just stand still. If I rest my hands on the kitchen counter to balance myself, and close my eyes, and just give in to every stab of pain and every wave of nausea. Just feel it all. Sometimes, if I do that, there's a moment when I feel it all with remarkable clarity, and somehow I don't mind how I feel. It's almost . . . *interesting* to me. Mysterious, and interesting."

That last part was a risk. I knew that as soon as I said it. Which is why I almost never speak about those moments of standing still, of pausing to ponder my pain, with anyone. Certainly not with doctors.

"But I can't stand still in my kitchen forever," I hurried to add. "And also, when I stand still like that, before long I know what will happen, what always happens, which is a rush like an airplane engine, and then a hollow ringing in my ears. The distinct sense that I'm going to faint."

I paused, and the young pain doctor said, "And what do you do then?"

I decided not to tell him everything; I left out the best solution, which has come from Tom. "I usually take several Advil and have a drink," I said. "And then I go to sleep."

He nodded, and at that point it was clear: he'd decided he knew exactly who I was and what I wanted. He had made a decision about me, a judgment. And it was not kind.

"You seem to have a rather deep and meaningful relationship with your pain," he said. And at that I stood up, avoiding his eyes, and I walked out of his office.

• • •

My phone pings now, at noon, and I look over to see that it's a message from Min. "Please call me," the message says.

For now, though, I am standing at my kitchen counter. My fingers rest lightly on its edge. The bourbon I've poured starts sweet on my tongue, then scours my throat and starts to loosen my shoulders the tiniest bit. I'll call her back soon, I think.

Because something has suddenly occurred to me. *I* could buy that farm, with or without Michael's involvement. In fact, I could buy it out from under him. I could move us all there and begin anew. I could become someone, or something else. Something closer, maybe, to the self I long ago abandoned. The self before this me of the past thirty years: this senseless, climbing vine, out of its element and rising, only rising— upwards to nowhere.

Dreamers

WHAT THEY GAVE TOM before the tube went in must have been good, because Min told him he woke up singing. Something about having a sweetheart and finding her faithless, she said. He'd have laughed, if he could have done such a thing with his mouth and throat stuffed full, to think how far back his dreams must have taken him. He'd woke up singing "After the Ball."

Which made Non smile—he'd seen her smiling at him. *I was singing with Non. She looked happier than I ever saw her!* And suddenly Min was gone.

But no, that had to be another time. Some other hospital, someplace else where Min had been his nurse. He's in the V.A. hospital now, with a tube down his throat. They brought him here in an ambulance. He'd been coughing so hard he thought he'd blow out his entire lungs. He was too weak to tell them not to take him to the V.A.

He'd have told them to take him to Hahnemann. But Hahnemann was closed, he remembers now. So maybe Temple. Anywhere but the V.A.

But then he found out Min is working here now.

Remind me, Min had said to him that other time, who was Non?

He'd been close to death then, for another reason. Maybe hypothermia, maybe an overdose, he'd been in for lots of reasons through the years. And of course before he knew

Min and didn't want to disappoint her, he'd gone in search of pain meds. Once he met Min in the E.R. at Hahnemann, instead of going elsewhere (the clinic in Fishtown, people were telling him at one point, though he'd never gone there), he kept going to Hahnemann. Just because he liked talking to Min. Even if he wasn't going to leave with a few Percocets in his pocket, because he didn't want her to think badly of him.

He told Min about the woman who took care of him when he was a child. One of his two pretend grannies, Non and Prue.

Now he's at the V.A. and Min's not his nurse. Or maybe she is; he can't really tell because people bustle around his bed all day and all night, but they keep their distance and they're dressed like astronauts. Min's here though; he's seen her, he knows he has. He's talked with her—or well, she's talked.

He wouldn't have chosen the V.A. But he'd had a coughing fit that left him gasping and gagging in front of the food pantry on Atlantic, and when the ambulance came someone said "He's a vet"—probably Sister Camila, thinking she was doing him a favor—and now here he is. The place where Min works now.

He'd dragged himself to the food pantry because he hadn't eaten anything in a couple days, and he'd thought maybe he'd try a can of soup. And maybe they'd have something for his pounding head. Also, he was going to need someplace else to stay. He'd been sleeping on a cot in the garage of a guy he knew, in exchange for work he was doing on the '76 Mustang that guy had just bought. But for the past couple of days every time he got up and tried to do some more work on the thing he'd had to immediately lie back down.

The guy had heard his coughing and said he'd have to go, that he was going to have to fumigate the whole goddamn garage now, and Tom had better get to the hospital. Hadn't Tom heard about this fucking virus, hadn't he seen all those people wearing masks, didn't he watch the fucking news? Tom just shrugged; it took too much energy to try to answer, to say no, he did *not* watch the fucking news. The fucking news just made him fucking depressed.

You should rest, he'd tried to tell Min with his eyes, because there was gauze or something stuffed in his throat. Take a walk in the sunshine; don't waste your precious time checking on me. Her own eyes through the plastic goggle things she wore were as dark and kind as he remembered from all those other times. But she looked tired, haggard really. Not like herself, he could see that, even through all that gear she had on.

She told him to relax, to be still. She tucked the sheet at his feet. She said, I told you you wouldn't go out that other time; I told you you'd kick it. And you did. And now you'll kick this, too.

He doesn't deserve this confidence, this young woman's steady thrum of kindness. No one does.

He'd done what she asked and closed his eyes. He'd tried to sleep.

He's not singing now. He couldn't if he tried. Every movement of his heaving lungs—hot air coursing in and out, a bellows stoking a fire—every way a song might travel has been stuffed with plastic tubes.

But no, that isn't true. He *is* in a hospital bed, but there's nothing in his mouth or nose. So maybe he dreamed that other time. Or did he? Or is this the time before that, and *are* these people from outer space that keep coming to read the computer screen and stare at him?

He'd been a fool when he was young; Non had told him as much. Go to Canada, she'd said. I'll give you the money. As if she had money to spare, tucked in that tiny room with everything she owned, which wasn't much. Open the window, she said that day, and when he did, she said can you smell it? She meant the lake, Lake Michigan, which to his mind had no smell.

You're thinking of the sea, he told her. The mighty Atlantic. That had been their joke: the Milfords and their mighty Atlantic. Looking toward Europe. Imagining themselves as lords and ladies, Non said, every one of them. All of them except Annie's daughter, the silent old maid with a limp, lingering in the shadows. Even the little brat, Robert's son, and his nervous slip of a mother, Annie's daughter-in-law.

She actually *was* English, that jittery young wife, Non said; she remembered that. How she ended up with that lout of a husband God only knew.

That lout of a husband was your Annie's son, Tom had thought that day, but he kept it to himself. Instead he said the other cousins weren't so bad, the ones from the first family, the first wife. Because they weren't really; they were good enough to him. He'd written to one of them, Larry, for some years after that. Larry's older sister Lucy was fourteen that summer, older than Tom, and once, at the edge of a bonfire on the beach, she'd taken his hand and led him to a spot below the boardwalk, then pulled down the top of her swimsuit to show him her breasts. A few years later Larry wrote that Lucy was in love with a soldier. Probably that's what had put the idea of enlisting in Tom's head, stupid, aimless kid that he'd been. That and not knowing what else he'd do, or where he'd go. It was that or be drafted, for someone like him.

He's slept again, he doesn't know for how long, and he wakes to see Min peering down at him. She's brought a letter she wants to read to him, she says. It'll crack him up, she says. It's from a woman who taught a poetry class she took in college, years ago.

"My dearest Minerva," she begins and rolls her eyes. "That's exactly how this woman talked in class," she says, shaking her head.

It's the first time he's heard that Min is short for Minerva. All those times she turned him or changed his bandages or emptied his bedpan, had he done all the talking then? Was it something they gave him? What made him tell her so much and ask her so little?

The letter has something to do with Min's mother. Mostly Min is laughing as she reads, getting all tangled up in this woman's ridiculous locutions. But he can see the tension in Min's forehead, the fear in her eyes, even behind the goggles.

Min laughed back when he told her he'd made his way to Philly by way of the Jersey shore. It's just that the Jersey shore was basically a joke by then, she told him, a dumb TV show, not exactly a destination site, and he didn't try to explain to her what it had meant to him sixty years ago, as a landlocked Irish Catholic kid from the northwest side of Chicago. That trip with Non was the first time he saw the ocean. He still remembers how he gagged and coughed, his chest ripped and scraped from the rocks and shells at the shoreline, the first time he tried to mimic his new friends, riding a wave with his skinny, freckled body.

Twelve years later, after his tour, Tom headed back to the Jersey shore. John, a guy from his platoon, was from Asbury

Park. He said they could get work on the boardwalk, repairing the amusement park rides. Another advantage of being a gearhead, forced to finish Catholic high school and skipping other classes to go work in the auto shop to make it through. He and John were mechanics; they'd worked on tank engines and gotten high. Which didn't mean he didn't see things he wanted to forget once he was back stateside. Because he did.

Not the kinds of things the vets he's met on the streets saw though. IEDs and severed limbs and heads blown completely off bodies, those kinds of things. These guys started with pain pills when they got back and then moved on from there. He'd have done the same if they'd offered, when he came back. Instead he and John just kept on the lookout for weed, other stuff when they could find it. John knew where to go.

In the E.R. another time Min took his vitals and said, I thought you said your buddy got you to Philly. I said he got me to the Jersey shore, he told her; a woman got me to Philly.

She'd laughed again then. Min had a full and rich laugh for such a small person. He didn't tell her that she reminded him of that woman in certain ways. Or that he'd hit that woman a few times, when he was blind drunk. Weed was better, for that reason, and so was smack. He behaved better then. When he saw what he'd done to her he gave up on booze. Not worth it. He wasn't looking to hurt anybody else. That wasn't the point.

She was a beautiful woman named Lisa—full-blooded Algonquin she told him once, but he doubted that—and he followed her to Philadelphia. Not too long after that she overdosed and died.

• • •

WAS MIN THERE when they put the tube in? He doesn't think so but he can't remember.

No, he thinks, she doesn't work here.

But yes, she does work here. Just not on the floor where he is. Which is where again? It isn't like the other times. He couldn't stop coughing and then he couldn't breathe and they'd brought him here in an ambulance. Here is the V.A. Which he keeps confusing with Hahnemann. But no, Min says, Hahnemann closed, remember? And then she reads him more of that woman's letter.

This woman, her professor, says she wants to help Min's mother somehow. He can't follow why.

Min rolled her eyes one more time, laughing at that part of the letter. Can you believe that? Can you believe she thinks my Uncle Eddie's going to sell the building to her? The one where my mom and my Uncle Pedro and his kids live? That he'd just kick them out for the price she's ready to offer?

But underneath the laughter and eye-rolling she sounds scared, Tom thinks. Like she doesn't really know why her uncle *wouldn't* sell the building.

This is serious. Tom thinks. This is a serious problem for Min, who has enough to deal with right now, wearing all those layers of protective gear and working round the clock and still managing to come check on him.

Is that what she's doing? Or is she somehow asking for his advice? He hopes to God she isn't doing that, asking for advice from him. What kind of fool would do that? Not Min. Surely not Min, no matter how exhausted and scared and fed up she is. That's how it seems to Tom, despite Min's laughter. That's she's just *done*. And it's unnerving. He's never seen her like this.

She shakes her head and lets out a little whistle and says *Jesus, these white ladies* under her breath. Then she laughs again.

It's odd, because Min never curses at work. Min never says *Jesus* like that around a patient. But maybe he's more than a patient. It flatters him really, to think that. To think that Min is sharing a joke with him right now.

But he can't shake the feeling that this isn't really funny. That there's something more going on with Min, or her mother, maybe both of them. But it's all blurry, the sounds, Min's face through her mask and goggles. His ears aren't filled with tubes, too, are they? Why does it feel like they are? Like every hole he's got is stuffed with gauze. Like he can't make anything look or sound clear. Like his ears and throat no longer work. Like there's nothing but the slow-burning fire in his chest, people from a science fiction movie hovering around him, long periods when things go dark, and then—at certain gold moments: Min. Her tired and worried eyes, her underwater voice. Reading that letter, which he cannot follow.

Sometimes, at Hahnemann, they talked about gardens. He asked Min to ask her mother, Raiza, for advice because he was helping at a community plot in Kensington. Trying to grow vegetables. Him, a gray-haired Irish mick from Chicago, acting like he was a farmer. How about that? But he'd watched Lisa make things root and rise from the dirt behind their half a double in Frankford, mostly scrub and weeds and rocks but she'd managed to grow tomatoes there, and beans, squash. One year some ears of corn. From Lisa he learned when to water and how much. And to put tobacco or coffee grounds or the tea from tea bags around the plants—a gift to them, and you had to tell them so, she'd said, and so he still did that, too, under his breath so no one would hear him and think he was a fool. And from Min, who asked Raiza, he learned what to do about the rats. Peppermint oil she said, and he'd found some—at a shop run by a woman he knew in Fishtown—and it worked. The rats went somewhere else, and that summer he gave away bushels of squash and tomatoes.

My mother knows a lot of things, Min told him.

Tell me some more of the things she knows, he asked her once, wanting to make her stay, wanting not to think about how bad it was going to be when they made him leave and it all started again, as it always did, everyone asking for his help, for pills, whatever he could get for them. Everyone needing him, leading him right back to where he started. Even Nina, his wealthy employer.

When you're sad or overwhelmed go looking for a garden. That was one thing Min's mother had taught her, she said. And another: Lie on your back and look at the sky. To find a patch of green she'd climbed the steep hill outside of Reading. There was a Chinese pagoda there, she told him, and Tom remembered, vaguely, going there once himself. She'd started climbing that hill when she was really little she said, laughing—and he'd thought to himself that he could listen to that sound, the soothing sound of Min's laughter, all day long. She was probably far too little, too young to be climbing a hill outside the city of Reading, she said. And then she shrugged and her eyes flashed. "But here I am. Nothing bad happened."

Nothing bad should ever happen to a person like Min. He knows this, and he also knows all the bad things that still *could* happen to her—because of who she is, something called "a dreamer" she told him, because her mother isn't legal and neither are her uncles, because of, well, there is no because. This is what he has known for a very long time. There is no because. There is just the way it is. The fucked-up, ridiculous way it is. The thing he was supposedly fighting for, and all the others since then too. He was shipped to Vietnam for one in a long row of lies. You could line them up like dominoes, and he had, a long time ago, and then kicked them and momentarily enjoyed the spectacle as they all came crashing down. But afterwards, there was nothing but dust and debris, and silence. A kind of death.

Tell me other things your mother told you, he said to Min another time. She'd been talking about the "dreamer" business and had grown quiet. Worried.

"Books are better for your brain than TV."

He'd nodded then. "This I know to be true," he said.

You can do fine with rice and beans if you keep some good greens growing year-round to add to them.

He would like to taste Raiza's food, he thinks now. He'd give a lot, if he had anything to give, to taste those greens.

"Watch for the first frost, but until then keep whatever you can outside. Lock it up if you have to."

"Talk to the plants the way you talk to children. Tell them what you're doing when you prune them or move them around."

"A man will leave, probably. Be sure you're strong enough on your own."

When Min talked about Raiza, Tom would find himself smiling. But when she talked about her old boyfriend Charlie, Nina's son, the guy who kept calling Min from the other side of the world, it was different. When Min talked about Charlie, Tom wanted to kill the guy.

He told her that once. But Min said, nah, it's okay. I don't mind when he calls now. He just needs someone to cheer him up and boost his ego a little bit.

That shrug again, the gleam in her eye.

He needed her way more than she needed him, she said. She'd figured that out a long time ago.

* * *

MIN, AND OTHER GOOD NURSES like her, talk to their patients the whole time they're with them. I'm going to lift you and turn you now. This tube has to be replaced; I'll do it as fast as I can; it shouldn't hurt much. The sores look a little better today. You're sleeping more; that's good.

Sometimes he pretended to be sleeping, just to hear what they would say if they didn't know he was awake. One nurse, he remembers, told him dirty jokes.

It was like how he talked to the plants, when no one was around. Let's just move you over here, where there's more sun. I'm just clipping your dead leaves, or nipping off some seeds; I'll save them so there's more of you.

He talked to the vegetables at the community garden, and to the flowers and ferns in Nina's yard. It had seemed to work, though probably it was just all the good rain they'd had the past couple years.

And yes, a man probably *will* leave. He'd been doing that to women since Non and Prue. Relying on them, needing them, and offering them basically nothing in return. Nothing but heartache.

But it wasn't true, what Non thought about that time she brought him along to Philadelphia and New Jersey, and then to DC. It wasn't true that he'd tipped his family off about Non and her lost love Annie. Back when they came back from the trip east, and his grandmother made him move in with her to get him away from Non and her influence. Her "deviant" influence was what the old bag had said specifically, and she'd made him move in with her and his so-called sister who was really his mother. Speaking of being deviant.

It wasn't him. He hadn't said a word. Even though he *did* know about it by then. He learned about it from Lucy; everyone on her side of the family knew the story, she said. How the old man, the patriarch, had snatched his crazy second wife away from a female lover in Chicago. It was all a shameful secret. And also fascinating, Lucy told him. Because now look at that woman, at his second wife. She's fat and drunk and miserable and nuts. And her children are as bad as she is.

He made sure to tell Non this, the day he came to see her before he left for basic training. The last time he saw her. She'd told him to open the window that day, to breathe in the air, the smell—though you could barely see the smallest corner of the blue lake, and there was nothing to smell but auto exhaust. Then they laughed about the Milfords and the mighty Atlantic, and he said I didn't tell them, you know. My family. I didn't say a word.

She'd looked at him for just a second, then looked down at the floor.

"How did they know then?" she'd asked him.

He hadn't said what he knew to be true. It was Prue. It was Prue who thought Non couldn't, or shouldn't, be with him once he was a teenager. That's what she told them. She never got over being furious about it, about the fact that Non had taken him away that summer. That she'd introduced him to the Milfords, to beer and cigarettes and Lucy's bare breasts below the boardwalk.

What if he'd listened to her, to his Non, to dear old deviant Maude? What if he'd taken the bit of cash she'd socked away and hitchhiked up to Canada? What might have happened then?

It's a ridiculous question. Ridiculous to think he'd have been any different. He'd still be a junkie, most likely. Always on the verge of sliding off the rails again.

Or, now, struggling to breathe on his own.

And he wouldn't have met Min. He wouldn't have become a decent gardener, even if he does it, now, on a weed-choked corner lot in Kensington that's littered with needles and condoms. And for a rich woman, who pays him—also thanks to Min.

"Charlie thinks he wants to save me," Min used to say to him. "Why do people like Charlie and Charlie's mom all think they're gonna save me somehow, when *they're* the ones on a high-speed train to hell?"

. . .

WHAT DAY IS IT when he wakes up this time? Min is there. She laughs again—that listless laugh that unnerves him—and tells him that each time she resumes reading the letter from her old college professor, he falls asleep.

It's like being a student in that woman's class, she says. Better than Ambien.

She has to get back to work but just wants to mention one thing to him, she says.

It does have to do with the letter. And with her mom, who's not doing so well. She's getting worse—wandering around Reading in her nightgown in the middle of the night, never taking a bath. It's more than her uncle and his girlfriend can handle. But if that woman, that professor named

Mary Stinson, *does* buy the building, Min says, where will my mom go?

He watches her closely, getting a bead on her eyes as best he can, and he sees something he's never seen in her before. She looks the way Lisa looked, not long before it happened. One of those overdoses that wasn't an accident. He knew that. Everyone who knew her did.

He tries to lift his hand but he can't. He wants to reach out to Min, wants to take her hand. Don't think this way, he wants to tell her. You can't do that. You can't give in.

She shakes her head and blows a quiet whistle through her teeth. Then she laughs, and it's low and bitter, nothing like the music of her laughter in the past.

Nina's texted her, she tells him, with a crazy idea. She was drunk when she wrote the message, of course. She said she wants to buy a farm. To grow grapes there and make wine. She thinks we should all move there—you, my mom, Charlie, me.

She's whispering this news to him, like it's a secret.

"What do you know about growing grapes, Tom?" Nina said to ask the next time she saw him, Min says, still whispering.

He smiles then, certain now that he's dreaming.

"Not a goddamn thing," he says, and he slides deeper into sleep.

• • •

THIS TIME HIS DREAMS are beautiful. This time there are arbors and trellises and fat blue grapes. Larger than any real grape has ever been. The sky is a dusty pink, a sunset sky, and everything around him is green and growing.

For some reason it smells like the ocean. Like the mighty Atlantic.

He stole a book from Non's room, that last time he visited her. Walt Whitman's *Leaves of Grass*—a favorite of hers, she'd read from it to him when he was a child. She was sure to have missed it immediately. She probably knew he took it.

Over the years since, he'd read it countless times; he'd pondered passages Non had marked.

Prodigal, you have given me love—therefore I to you give love!
O unspeakable passionate love.

He has the book still, tucked in a pocket of the Army surplus pack where he keeps his clothing and a few valuables. He wonders where that pack is now.

He'd planned to return the book to Non one day. But she'd died before he got there, and he didn't attend her funeral. He hasn't been back to Chicago since he left at eighteen.

Non died quietly, Prue wrote in a letter afterwards, while reading a different book. Prue didn't say which one.

How could he have missed it before? That this is who Min is: someone who will give and give until she dies from all the giving. Like Non.

But, better that than giving in early, too early. Like Lisa.

It pains him to do it, but it's the only option he has. When Min returns—did she ever leave?—he turns away from her. He lets her know that his answer is no. No to moving to a farm outside Reading. No to growing grapes for her boyfriend's mother.

There's no way to tell Min what he wishes he could say: You can't give in. *You* have to take care of your mother, and all these sick and dying people in the hospital too. You have to keep caring. Even if it kills you, eventually. That's where we're all headed eventually, after all.

Tom never gave in before, though at times he came close. But he will now. He will now because it's the right thing to do. For Min. And because he can hear Non singing "After the Ball"—*Many a heart is aching, if you could read them all*—and not in her wavery old woman's voice, but in the voice he can almost remember from when he was a child. A strong and deep, full-throated voice, her voice for the stage.

He can hear her singing, and it sounds like she's very close, maybe in the next room, with the wind blowing through the open window, stirring the curtain near her face. Just as he remembers her.

He knows how strong Min is, truly. She'll be all right, she'll make it through. And he wants to sing with Non one more time. So he concentrates on breathing in, as deep and long as he can one last time. And then he lets go.

Indifferent History

DEAR MIN—or should I say, dearest Minerva,
 I write to express my grave concern for your mother Raiza at this time of global pandemic. Perhaps you are aware that the members of your family who share the building where she lives in Reading have not, for quite some time (if at any time), practiced social distancing. To my knowledge they have never worn masks. Raiza eats little, I know, and seldom leaves her own apartment or rear garden. But when she does, I fear for both her safety and her health. And so I am writing to ask you, dear Min, dearest Minerva—no, not to ask, to *urge* you—to persuade your mother to allow me to help.
 I am aware that you cannot return to your mother's apartment now. That as a nurse, though you are tested daily, you could put others at serious risk. Particularly someone Raiza's age and with her clearly weakened lungs. My wish for your mother is a quiet life in a more peaceful, bucolic setting. A place, perhaps, where her garden might grow beyond the dozen pots she crowds onto her tiny patio in the summer and then into her equally small kitchen in the winter. In fact, I am prepared to offer her a home in the so-called mother-in-law apartment that is attached to my home, which is located in a quiet rural hamlet ten miles outside the city of Reading.

This will be possible for her, if she is able to persuade her brother, your Uncle Eddie, to sell the building on 13th Street to the county historical society, where I will assume the mantle of president in the coming year.

Let me say a bit more by way of explanation.

I've only recently learned of our connection, and the circumstances of my doing so will likely surprise you. You were my student in a college poetry class perhaps ten years ago; do you recall it? I remember you as rather quiet, but with a spark of life when we read certain poets who were also favorites of mine. I believe you wrote a paper about Naomi Shihab Nye's "Yellow Glove," a work I also love (that closing line—"Part of the difference between floating and going down"—it haunts me still!).

So imagine my surprise when I discovered that a relatively new friend of mine, Raiza Perez, is your mother.

I met your mother in a rather unusual way—which is to say I simply waited outside her building one day until she came out the door and then essentially pounced on her! Yes, this alarmed her, but soon I explained my presence, and she grew interested. Let me say that you are the daughter of a lovely woman, and the resemblance is strong. Though I might not have noticed it immediately, had I not seen the many photographs of you that adorn the walls of her apartment. Including your college graduation photo; the moment I saw it, I practically screamed, "I *know* this girl!"

But perhaps she has shared the story of our meeting with you by now. In fact, I'm sure she has—it was so unusual, and yes, rather brazen, for someone like me to approach a woman like your mother in the way that I did. But so I did, and for reasons you probably already know, it occurs to me.

Because you are such a lovely, devoted daughter, I know that you speak to your mother by phone nearly every day.

I'm certain she shares details about her life with you, so perhaps you've heard about me. I *am* concerned that she may not be sharing enough about her life, however, especially of late. But more on this in a moment.

What I needed dear Raiza to understand is that she resides in a special place—one rich in local history. But rich in the kind of local history that has, unfortunately, been routinely ignored. I am speaking specifically of Elsie Kachel Stevens, the wife of the esteemed modernist poet Wallace Stevens. She was a lovely young woman when the great W met her—quiet and musical, and also poor, from the wrong side of the tracks. But don't be mistaken: Despite how the residents of Reading and the surrounding suburban enclaves might view South 13th Street now (and yes, I am aware that there is contempt for immigrant communities among some in our fair county, and even a reconstituted county jail that's now a site for detaining and separating immigrants only a few miles outside our fair city, along a winding country road that smells of freshly cut grass—the kind of place old W himself would have waxed nostalgic for during his years of peddling insurance policies in stuffy old Connecticut), the street where your mother and her brother and his wife and children now live would have been, in Elsie Kachel's day, solidly middle class.

But even then, South 13th Street wouldn't have lived up to the standards of Wallace Stevens's family. His parents, Kate and Garrett, refused to attend the wedding when W married Elsie, considering her beneath their son. The Stevens family lived on 5th Street, in a building that now houses the offices of a law firm, though—based on the less than lovely upkeep (dust and leaves always blown up against the door, straggling blades of grass poking up through gaps in the sidewalk's stone)—perhaps not a very successful one.

I have, in recent years, endeavored to restore the reputation of Elsie Kachel (sometimes called Elsie Kachel Moll, though not by me, because her mother's second husband, Lehman Moll, never adopted Elsie). History has not been kind to her, as it tends not to be to the wives of famous men. Or if not unkind, history has been, at best, indifferent to the selfless and neglected wives of "great men." (History itself, I believe, must be a man—rather like my deceased husband, a professor of history at the college you attended: Herbert Stinson. His field was classics. I only wonder if you might have known of him because of your dear mother's love of the ancient Greeks and Romans; hence your marvelous name!).

In Elsie's case, history has definitely been unkind. Unkind and completely unfair. As were her husband and their daughter. Elsie is depicted as a depressive, even perhaps a madwoman—a drain on her husband's resources and emotional energy. A religious obsessive. A reader of middle-brow literature with no capacity to appreciate her husband's genius.

Never mind that she was a master gardener, a careful and scrupulous editor of her husband's letters (I will argue to my grave that she edited out his likely infelicities—not instances of sexual frankness, as certain critics have maintained). She was also the model for the Mercury dime!

That's right. As sculptor Adolph Weinman's model for a bronze bust he created in 1913, Elsie wore a Phrygian cap with wings. Weinman meant for the wings to symbolize liberty of thought, but Americans seem to have confused his goddess Liberty with the Roman god Mercury. Hence the name, "the Mercury dime"—perhaps the most famous item in the history of American coinage, one that became part of the culture. Think "Brother, Can You Spare a Dime." Think of the lowbrow nineteenth-century American entertainments known as dime museums. Think of polio and the March of Dimes.

In short, there is a need for more than a historical marker on South 13th Street, in my opinion. I have come to this conclusion after years of research into the life of Elsie Stevens, but also into the life of another long-forgotten woman, Laura Leggett Barnes, wife of the famous Philadelphia art collector Albert Barnes. Laura Barnes was a contemporary of Elsie Stevens, and, like Elsie, a master gardener. She was also childless—which, considering the Stevens's daughter Holly's ultimate loyalties, may have been a blessing. Like Elsie, Laura has been completely overlooked, if not derided, by history.

These two women were to be the focus of my doctoral dissertation, begun when Herbert and I met as graduate students in the 1970s, at a large, land-grant university that I elect not to name. Suffice it to say that said university seized the opportunity afforded by Ronald Reagan and the 1980s to defund its fledgling women's studies program, a loss it has only recently begun to rectify. This delayed correction is the main reason said university will never see a *dime* of my money. (Note, again, how the dime litters our vernacular!)

For a while, I pursued another possible line of research, into the life of Olga Rudge: musically accomplished mistress to, and emotional supporter of, the rabid anti-Semite Ezra Pound. This work took me down some very interesting paths. Did you know, for instance, that a recent gift establishing a beautiful poetry wing at an already lavishly funded private library in Chicago was offered on condition that the wing be named for two completely unknown women—surnames Garrett and Davies—one of whom was the mother of the donor? And that, at the height of the Modernist period in American poetry, these two women lived together in a Chicago boarding house, in what has been euphemistically termed a Boston marriage? And that one of them did, in fact, know Ezra Pound? But none of these women—not the donor, and neither of the women whom she honored with her gift—seems to have written a line of poetry herself; I have searched and searched, to no avail. More's the pity. And the truth is, over time spent following the paths of these two women for whom the library wing is named to the inevitable dead end, I simply lost interest in both Olga Rudge *and* Pound's long-suffering and ultimately estranged wife Dorothy Shakespear. Both were fascist enablers, honestly; why pursue them further?

A brief aside: I'm sure you're aware of Gertrude Stein's famous dismissal of Ezra Pound as the "village explainer—excellent if you were a village, but if you were not, not." But perhaps you may not have heard of the lesser-known observation of the poet H.D., who had a brief love affair with Pound when both were quite young: "One would dance with him only for what he might say." Apparently, he was a dreadful dancer, which perhaps says all one needs to know about his insufferable poetry.

I stopped pursuing *all* of these women's stories, for quite some time. And then—in short—the world of women's studies became the world of critical gender studies, forging ahead without me. It's an old story really, one you may have heard (though one that will not in any way speak to your situation, dear Min, practical twenty-first-century woman with a career in nursing that you are). Man meets woman; both have lofty intellectual ambitions. Woman's ambitions, unfortunately, lie within a poorly understood and financially vulnerable field of inquiry. Woman also becomes pregnant, with the first of two children. Man completes degree and acquires tenure-track position at a small college in Pennsylvania; woman tags along, raises said children, and teaches countless sections of freshman composition—and, when the department occasionally decides to throw her a bone, an introductory course in American Poetry. Man—by now an embittered and alcoholic former scholar who believes, to his dying breath, that he was robbed of the academic acclaim he deserved—eventually dies. Woman's dissertation research molders. Woman takes up with the local historical society, one of her "pet projects," in the words of the Man. Whom, every time he uttered that phrase over the course of their last twenty years together, the Woman imagined smothering in his sleep.

But I should return to my original purpose in writing to you. To wit: my "pet project" with the county historical society has expanded to include the possible purchase of Elsie Kachel's childhood home and the establishment of a new Pennsylvania Women's History Society office and exhibit space there.

We are at work on securing a state historical landmark designation for the building and launching a capital campaign. Something like what the Barnes Foundation has done for Albert Barnes and his collection in Philadelphia. (Once again ignoring Laura.) Do not be fooled: There is money in our sleepy little city and its surroundings as well. Generational wealth exists here, even in our under-the-radar, post-industrial, and rural corner of the world. Not on the scale of Philadelphia's cultural and philanthropic elite, perhaps. But enough to pay your Uncle Eddie a handsome price for his building. And to make possible a better life—a safer life, a more expansive life—for your dear mother.

I hope you will assist me in this endeavor, dearest Minerva. I await your reply at the number, email address, or mailing address above.

Yours sincerely, and with genuine regards and affection,
M. S.

P.S. I enclose, for your reading pleasure (I do recall how fervently you read and responded to certain poems in my class!), a portion of my play about Elsie Kachel Stevens and Laura Legget Barnes, titled *Unexceptional American Love Stories*. The title comes from a line by critic Milton J. Bates in his article "Stevens in Love: The Woman Won, the Woman Lost": "They coped with disillusionment in the fashion their generation approved—he by remaining a devoted husband, she by remaining a loyal wife. Theirs was not, in the last analysis, an exceptional love story."

Do please let me know what you think!

Tenderness

MIN SITS ON THE CURB outside the hospital, stretching her legs in front of her. Her feet are beyond aching, beyond the way they used to hurt at the end of a round of clinicals when she was just a student. Now they're just numb. Everything is numb. She forgets, really, how her feet, or any other part of her body, is supposed to feel. Her feet's only function is to propel her from place to place, patient to patient. Numbest of all is her brain, or her heart (which also means her brain of course), the part that's supposed to feel something.

The parking lot is still eerily empty, but cars are buzzing by on University Avenue, and the air smells of auto exhaust again. That had stopped for a while, at the beginning of the lockdown. Blue skies, clean air, a quiet like she could not recall experiencing except for one time, the time she and Charlie drove north on a whim in the springtime, putting up a borrowed tent and camping in the Pocono Mountains for two nights.

It's almost 9:00 A.M., she's in the state of permanent exhaustion that is her life now, and she should go home and go to bed. But instead she sits at the edge of the parking lot, watching a bird that's landed just a few feet away from her and thinking about a poem she read in college.

Back when she took Dr. Stinson's class she preferred the poems that weren't about love. Dr. Stinson had told the class they could call her Mary, but no one did. She was the age of their grandmothers after all, and it felt weird to call her by her first name.

Dr. Stinson was odd, and kind of annoying, but still Min had felt a spark of rage when Charlie made fun of her. Where did he get off doing that? The woman had a Ph.D., for God's sake. What did he have, besides his family's money?

But everyone in the department mocked her, Charlie said. She was just so earnest, so deadly serious about the trials of women writers. Which was true. And honestly, the poem Min liked best, because it started out seeming like it would be another love poem but then it wasn't, it went in a completely different direction, was by a man named Philip Levine. "Smoke," it was called, and Min liked it because it told a story, as all the poems she liked did.

Min likes old men's stories, maybe because she hasn't really known very many old men. She met her grandparents, her mother's parents, only once, on a long-ago trip to the D.R. when she was five, and all she recalls about them are her grandmother's sternness and her grandfather's shrinking silence. Raiza, her mother, was clearly fond of her father, but even with her he barely spoke.

Min liked when her older patients were chatty and told her stories; they were happier and easier to distract, and help. Especially the men, and especially Tom. But now Tom is dead. He didn't make it through the night, she was told when she went to the Medical ICU to see him at the end of her shift. There was already someone else in his bed.

She still remembers a few things about that poem. The guy who wrote it was one of three male poets that Dr. Stinson was willing to have on her syllabus, she told them; all the rest were women. Min's forgotten the names of the other two men, who Charlie said were "just okay."

The poem started out being about a blind date between some guy's parents, a story the guy tells while he and several others are waiting for a bus. And that guy, the poet—but no, not necessarily the poet, "the speaker," Dr. Stinson taught them to say—understood the way the moon worked for the first time on that day he's remembering and talking about. The way the moon seems to come and go, but what's really going on with that, the way the earth is actually moving in relation to the moon. And Min remembers that part because it made her think of the thing that had happened to her during clinicals that semester, the way it had dawned on her, for the first time, that no one would be there with her in those hospital rooms once she graduated. That she'd be moving among those sick and dying people without a supervisor to lean on. Somehow it hadn't quite registered with her yet, the fact that she was going to be a solitary planet, making those rounds on her own. The realization had terrified her, but also thrilled her.

Not that there wouldn't still be know-it-alls around her all the time. Like Bailey, one of Tom's nurses in Med ICU. Bailey's sure all the Covid-19 patients, at least the intubated ones, hallucinate.

"You can't tell me that man's not back in Vietnam," she'd said about Tom once the tube went in and his eyes started darting around the room.

That's because no one can tell you anything, Min thought. She'd worked with Bailey before she got moved to Trauma. And anyway, if he's back in Vietnam in his head, good for him, Min thought. In that case he probably thinks he's high.

She'd caught the eye of another nurse, Loretta, and together they raised their eyebrows, the closest thing you could do to rolling your eyes with everything hidden behind a mask and goggles. Loretta, who was older and had been in the military herself, was someone Min knew to trust, and she was relieved Loretta was there, also caring for Tom.

Wherever Tom was, his nurses usually fell in love with him, sort of. He had that effect on people. He made no particular demands, other than always nudging for more painkillers. His interest in you was genuine, his kindness sincere. And the older nurses thought he was handsome; they said he looked like Clint Eastwood, the old, craggy-faced Clint Eastwood of today.

The speaker in that Philip Levine poem and the guys he's with see a little black bird in the gutter while they're waiting for the bus, and they think maybe it's injured. Someone uses the word "tenderness" while he talks about the bird, a word the speaker holds on to because it's one he's never used.

Min has recalled that poem now, sitting here on the curb, because the little bird that landed near her keeps flying away and then coming back, and now it's standing still and looking at her. Not injured, just curious. She recalls another thing about the poem: One of the guys thinks the bird is a baby grackle that's maybe lost. A baby grackle must be black, because another guy in the poem thinks the bird's a crow (a "context clue" is what Mary Stinson called that). But this bird, the one that's landed near Min, is brownish-gray. It has intelligent eyes.

Maybe it's come to tell her something about death, Min thinks, remembering that word again. *Tenderness.* It's a word she also never uses. There's been precious little tenderness in her life for a while now, especially since the virus showed up in Philadelphia.

Maybe Tom's spirit has arrived in this bird, which just keeps on watching her. Tom's tender spirit. *So now what will you do?* This is what the bird seems to be asking her. Since I won't be here to help with that crazy plan of Nina's. Since you're going to have to keep on doing what you're doing. Since you can't just walk out of the hospital and over to Baltimore Avenue and right into traffic, not now. That, or however you were thinking you might do it.

Because of course Tom had recognized what was happening to her. That she was honestly pondering it. That she's so tired of everybody dying, and no one doing anything about it really, and the exhaustion of this work and the worry about her mother and the ridiculous people like Mary Stinson and Charlie's mom Nina all thinking they understand her situation and can help.

So her old professor thinks she can just set Raiza up in her empty mother-in-law apartment, one that's probably filled with books, that's probably how she thinks she'll lure Raiza there. Okay fine: Who's going to take care of her once she's there? And what about the rest of the family? What about Pedro and his roving band of kids and grandkids? What's supposed to happen to all of them if Uncle Eddie accepts her offer and kicks them all to the curb? There will be no mother-in-law apartment for them at Dr. Stinson's place, or at Eddie and Brenda's place, that's for sure.

Suicide is a sin. Suicide is also poetic. Charlie used to talk about it but not mean it, she always knew that. Min hasn't wanted to talk about it at all. She thinks back over her last conversations with Tom, which weren't really conversations—just her talking to him, though she could tell he was hearing her. Had she said something about that to him, even as kind of a joke? Had she said what she was thinking out loud? *Maybe I'll just walk out the door and keep on going till I walk right into traffic on Baltimore Avenue. Maybe that's the solution.*

She's sure she'd only thought it, not said it. Because she also recalls thinking that wouldn't be the best way to try because if she did that she probably wouldn't die, and then she'd end up in the very place she was hoping to escape, and she'd be of no help to her mother then. She'd just be one more big part of the problem in this place.

It didn't bother her at first, the realization that she would work this hard for the rest of her life. Maybe take a few beach vacations through the years. Maybe have a couple babies and watch them grow up and wait for them to give her grandchildren, but never stop working this hard. At first she'd thought, well, all right then, bring it on. Because she did like the work. Then. Before this. Before all the senseless dying. Before watching them shove the tube down Tom's throat and thinking that that has seemed to kill more people than it's helped. But what did she know? Maybe he'd make it, she'd thought at first. Maybe they would all be saved by a rich person's escape plan—she'd actually considered it, briefly. Or maybe she could just be someone's private nurse or work in a school or something. Things she never would have considered before.

Raiza is growing senile, or so it seems. Everyone sees it, it might have been news to Mary Stinson, but Min and her uncles and cousins have been aware of this for a while now.

Or maybe she was always crazy. That's Uncle Eddie's hypothesis. Shy and bookish practically from the day she was born and then, of all things, falling for a Haitian cane cutter, pregnant (with Min) at nineteen and sent to live with her brothers in—fittingly—someplace called Reading, Pennsylvania, to escape the family's shame.

No point in explaining to the older generation back in the D.R., that you don't pronounce it that way: *Read-ing*, like the thing you do with books. It's *Redding.* Like the railroad. Like in Monopoly.

Four months ago, at a Christmas party at his house, Uncle Eddie had pulled Min onto his back deck for a private conversation. It was weirdly warm, fifty degrees or more, but she shivered in her ugly holiday sweater.

"You need to do something about your mother," he'd said. "A nursing home or something, I don't know."

"Very helpful of you," she'd said under her breath, not really caring if he heard her. She wasn't afraid of him anymore, not like she was when she was a kid. Eddie the patriarch, Eddie the big success, the big man who bought old houses in and around Reading and flipped them, doing much of the work himself, the big man in Reading who no one messed with and Min's mother Raiza revered.

Why was he suggesting a nursing home to her, when he was the one with money, and connections all over the city? He was the one who would know what to do about that; he had just put his mother-in-law in some kind of place, they'd all grumbled about it, Uncle Pedro and his girlfriend Shayla, some of their friends. All that money, that giant house, look how they live, but they lock the old woman up in a nursing home instead of taking care of her?

Not that Pedro and Shayla, with their gang of kids and grandkids always moving in and out of the second and third floor apartments of Eddie's building, had room to talk, really. It's not like they were handling everything so well. Pedro working shitty restaurant jobs and coming home drunk more nights than not, Shayla doing God knows what all day long, two kids in jail for selling drugs, grandkids always in trouble at school, when they actually got there.

Say what you want about Min's absent-minded mother: Raiza had managed to dress and feed Min and get her to school every single day. She'd been interested in what Min was learning. She'd cared for her diligently. Min knew that. Min also knew she'd never be able to put her mother in a home. Raiza had worked in housekeeping at Reading Hospital throughout Min's childhood, all the way through her years in college; she'd cleaned every single floor in that place. That's why she'd encouraged her daughter to become a nurse. She knew what the nurses made, the nice apartment complexes they lived in. That's what she'd wanted for Min. Something better, A real patio maybe, maybe even a yard. A full-size garden.

Of course no one blamed Eddie for putting his mother-in-law in a home. They blamed his wife Brenda. For the same reason Eddie expects Min to deal with Raiza on her own. She's the daughter. It's her job.

"You know I can't afford a nursing home," she'd said to him finally. "And she would hate that. And right now I can't take care of her. I'm working double shifts all the time, nights, I wouldn't be able to keep an eye on her, and she'd be miserable if I moved her out of her place."

And now there was this other reality, which is that Min is a walking Petri dish; she'd bring home all kinds of nasty things, but worst of all this virus. Which would probably kill her mother.

Eddie had stamped out his cigarette on a redwood plank of his spotless patio, then picked up the butt to add to a coffee can hidden below a chair. He shook his head. For maybe the hundredth time he said to her, "It could have been different for you, you know." If she'd stayed with Charlie, he means. If she'd gotten that hefty piece of the American pie. Like any sensible woman would have done. Like Brenda had done, with him.

Maybe Raiza *has* always been crazy, and this is the point it's come to. Other than her asthma, her lungs that have been wrecked by smoking and bad air, there's nothing else that's medically wrong with Min's mother. No recognizable source for dementia. Min has checked her regularly ever since she started nursing classes, listening to her heart, taking her blood pressure, getting her to the clinic for lab tests; there are plenty of doctors in her life now, ones who'll write the scrips for that. But whatever the reason, Raiza has started roaming the streets of Reading in the middle of the night, often in her nightgown. So far when the police have found her they have brought her home. But it's dangerous in a new way now. Her lungs won't make it through if she gets this virus. She'll have a tube rammed down her throat in a heartbeat.

At the thought of her mother—too skinny and too graying for a woman who's only forty-seven—in a sterile hospital bed, being intubated, a harsh and unexpected sob wracks Min's body.

Seeing the way she's suddenly trembling from her head to her Crocs-shod feet, the bird flies away.

Or maybe it was scared away by the man who's cast a shadow over Min now. She looks up to see Neel Amin, the neurology resident who so obviously wants to have sex with her again. If you're a "hot young thing," in Bailey's words, "there are plenty of docs who want to fuck you." Min is too dark for a lot of them, but not for Amin; she saw his interest the minute he showed up to check on a patient on her unit a month ago.

She'd thought she might enjoy it, that there might be some comfort in it, or at least some kind of release. Neel is tall and strong, really good-looking, a child of immigrants, like her; his parents are from Bangladesh.

He smirks too much though, like all the residents do—giving you this smug half-smile that lets you know they kind of pity you, really, for how little you know, how sad your small life must be. They have this built-in, superior way of looking at people—nurses, aides, their patients, too. It must be part of their training. But Neel isn't smirking now. He looks concerned as he sits next to her on the curb, though she suspects he's mostly faking it.

"You okay?" he asks. "Did you just lose someone?"

And for some reason she finds herself telling him about Tom. Defying all the HIPAA regulations, of course, but who's going to care about that on behalf of someone like Tom?

There's no logic to her sudden, wrenching mourning. Just as there was no logic to her friendship with Tom. It wasn't a friendship really, not exactly. They saw each other rarely, and only in hospitals where she worked. He was sometimes brought to the E.R. Earlier on, when she was still at Hahnemann, sometimes he brought himself. A bed, a place to warm up, and—if he hit the right time, the right rookie resident—some meds to help him sleep, and maybe to sell. This was better than what was on the streets, of course, so Min and the other nurses, or at least some of them, didn't really hold it against Tom. He was also a vet after all.

Tom was so much older than those others. He was so not the kind of person who should have been Min's friend. An old white guy, a Vietnam vet. But he wasn't what you expected. He was a good listener, he was curious. He was also a gardener. Like Raiza, and like Nina.

He shouldn't have died. Not yet. And not just because he was supposed to somehow set Min free. She leaves that part out as she talks to Neel. She leaves out the fact that she's been pondering an exit, a permanent one. Tom was supposed to be part of that plan too.

"So this guy was kind of like a grandfather to you maybe?" Neel says to her. She's surprised by the question, because Min was sure he wasn't listening as she talked about Tom. Most of the time he was looking at his phone, not even pretending to pay attention.

Not at all, she'd thought.

But "Yeah, well maybe, I don't know . . ." she'd said. "I don't think I would have put it that way. He was more like a friend. I know that probably seems weird."

Neel's phone dings with a text alert, and he looks relieved when he says "I gotta go."

He holds out a hand to help her up but she shakes her head. "I just want to sit here a little longer," she says.

He shrugs. "Suit yourself," he says. "But you really should go home and try to get some sleep. When are you off next? Wanna grab some carry-out and come to my place?"

Of course he still has time to ask about that before he rushes back to the hospital. That text was probably from his mother or something.

"Maybe," is all she'll offer. "I still have to sort out my schedule. I don't even know when I'm due back at this point—"

But he's halfway to the entrance by then, waving back at her. "Call me," he yells in her general direction.

And then, suddenly, the bird is back. It's the same one, she's sure of it, tilting its head to look at her again, one big black eye trained on her.

For some reason this bird doesn't remind her of Tom. It reminds her of Charlie. Who'd also liked that poem called "Smoke." Who'd told her he liked it because he liked stories about people that surprised you. That there could have been tenderness like that, concern about an injured bird, among a group of auto workers waiting for a bus. It reminded him, Charlie told her, of the rare occasions when Nina, his mother, talked about her childhood. How lonely and isolated she'd felt, but how her mother had bought her books. How pretty the sunsets were on the farm she'd grown up on. And once, when she was drunk, she told him how she'd really only grown embarrassed by that farm when she was in college and saw it for the first time through the eyes of Charlie's father.

The bird pecks at something in the dust; is there a bug there? Something growing in the dirt in the gutter that it wants to eat? Why does it keep hanging around?

This is the thing. Charlie *was* compassionate. He didn't fake that, it was real.

Another memory: Charlie rubbing her feet, that first semester of clinicals. They'd get dinner together, then go to his place, and before they started studying he'd fill a bucket with warm water and Epsom salt so she could soak her aching feet. She was bone-tired after those first days on the hospital floors. Bone-tired and kind of shell-shocked. It was hard at first, seeing what she saw. Old people pissing themselves, kids with deep cuts and bruises, people of all ages moaning in pain.

How did he even know about soaking your feet in Epsom salt, she'd asked him.

"My mom used to fill a pan for my great aunt," he told her. "Right up till the day she died."

His mom again, Nina, who'd always seemed to Min so self-involved, back when she first knew her. Though recently, sleeping in the guest suite in Nina's house in the early days of this crisis or whatever it is, this virus hell with no end in sight,

Min just did her best to avoid the woman. Nina's loneliness and neediness were just too much for her. She has no time and no patience for these rich and lonely white ladies, with their plans and schemes that people like Min and Tom are supposed to help them with now.

"She just doesn't know what to do with herself," Charlie said one time. "That's why she drinks, I think. She doesn't really know who she is, now that Liliane is dead, and I'm gone."

So Charlie had done what a rich white son apparently gets to do when his mother gets too needy: He packed a bag and headed to Europe.

Back in college, after her feet were soaked and soothed and they'd closed their books and gotten ready for bed, Min usually got keyed up again. Anxious about the next day, worried about all those suffering people. He'd invite her to tell him about it, what she was dreading, and then he'd rub her feet again, massage her legs and her shoulders, kiss her breasts, gently go down on her, soothing and distracting her until she came, clinging to him for life. And then she'd fall into a deep and dreamless sleep.

The things that had upset her back then, during clinicals. Old people with no one who came to visit, skinny little kids with broken bones, all of it so trivial compared to this, to what she's seeing now, every day. All these people competing for ventilators, coughing and gasping for air, crying for someone to come for them, to hold their hands. How would she even begin to try to describe to Charlie the life she's living now?

She's been with a few guys in the time she and Charlie have been broken up—Neel, a guy she knew in high school who's now in grad school at Penn, a P.A., Marlin, who sometimes works with her in the Trauma ICU. But no one has made her feel heard, and cared for, in the way that Charlie did. This much is true.

But Charlie remains on the other side of the world, doing God knows what, getting into fights and screwing other girls. Presumably no closer to figuring out his life than he'd ever been. She doesn't really know. He hasn't called her for a while.

And now, maybe he's invited to join his mother on a farm outside Reading, growing grapes and making wine, with Tom running that part of the operation.

So much for that plan, Nina, Min thinks. Your grape farmer didn't make it.

Suddenly, inexplicably, she is weeping again. For Tom, but also for Nina, whose son only comes home from Italy to renew his visa and then leaves her again. Maybe he's fallen in love with someone new. Maybe Min's crying for herself, too; maybe she was wrong to give up on Charlie. Maybe they could have made it work somehow.

Crying even for Mary Stinson. For all the sheltered, naive women who think they can help, that they can make a difference somehow. Poor old Dr. Stinson, with her lost dreams and all her feelings of emptiness and betrayal. Still trying to educate Min. It's like she can't help herself. Telling Min all about "generational wealth" in America. As if Min needs a lesson on that topic.

Uncle Eddie will never sell the building to Mary Stinson and her historical society. She'll never be able to offer him enough; he owns it outright, Min and Pedro pay the utilities, and where would they all go if he sold it? Uncle Eddie's not going to try to find them someplace else to live, not now, in the middle of this mess. Things are too easy for him right now, the way they are.

And probably no one will ever read, or see, Mary Stinson's sad play about sad, forgotten women married to important men. Which is too bad really, because some of the lines are really kind of nice. Min had to admit that, when she read them. *A woman who does not bear children is a kind of shed husk in autumn*, the wife of the art collector says. *A fading shadow behind the man she follows, still.* And the poet's wife quoting Sappho: "*Sweet mother, I cannot weave my web, broken as I am by longing.*"

Now Min is sorry she didn't read those lines to Tom. She imagines his eyes settling and his breath slowing as she read them. Since Dr. Stinson's letter arrived, Min has been repeating certain fragments as she worked, the way she'd repeated lines from some of the poems they read in class to distract herself when she had to dress a wound or change someone's soiled bedding during rounds in college.

Heading west, just like the sun, hidden in smoke. The last line from that Philip Levine poem—which, for a while, she and Charlie used to say to each other in the morning, before they kissed and headed off to class.

She's going to have to tell Nina about Tom somehow, sometime. But she can't face that now. She'll text her later, she decides.

One last probing look at Min, and the bird flies away again. Min rises slowly, too tired to think about any of it anymore. She pats her pocket and finds her keys, walks to her car, gets in, and starts the engine. She doesn't even bother to go back inside for her bag. She points the car toward West Philly, hoping to stay awake until she gets back to her apartment.

Maybe she'll call Neel when she wakes up, she thinks as the engine finally coughs to life. If she wakes up. Or maybe she'll take something and just forget about her next shift.

Maybe she'll sleep and sleep and finally dream this time; she hasn't dreamed about anything, or anyone, for weeks. About her mother when she was younger, maybe, her broken-toothed smile, laughing as she read Dr. Seuss books to Min. Or about Charlie carrying her little cousins on his shoulders. The thrill of being noticed by this tall, tatted guy whose curly blonde hair was always falling in his eyes as she sat in a hidden corner of the student union, studying between classes. How she'd offered to trim his hair the first time he talked to her, just because she wanted to touch it. And how gentle he was with her, how tender, always.

As she makes the turn onto 40th Street, a shadow crosses her windshield. Maybe it's that bird, she thinks, delirious with exhaustion. Or maybe it's Tom, with some angel wings now, flying overhead, following her as she drives. Keeping an eye on her. Making sure she gets home safe, and then gets back to work.

CODA

Those Who Can

PRAGUE, OCTOBER 2021

THE GIRL IS PLAYING A VIOLIN for change, outside Hlavni station. Here the police are less likely to harass her, Stefan supposes, though there would be far more tourists to busk for at the bridge or the clock tower. The tourists are back in Prague again, throwing their measly crowns into performers' cups. A one-crown coin is less than a twentieth of a euro; if you're American, it's between a penny and a nickel. But these tourists have no clue about that. They use credit cards and, when they have to in some of the shops, euros. When they get change in Czech crowns there's nothing to do with that but throw it in some performer's or beggar's cup.

All those battered old Czech crown coins that the people refuse to part with, passing from musicians' cases to breakdancers' caps to newsstand tills and then cycling around again. Like American pennies and nickels and dimes, his American friend Charlie said once when they were drinking and talking late into the night, tossing American quarters and Czech crowns into their empty glasses. What is even the point of continuing to mint the things? Charlie had wondered aloud. That was when Stefan had delivered his lecture on the gold standard. It embarrasses him to recall that now.

What a pathetic bore he'd become by then, still under the influence of those guys he'd met in Rome.

Outside the station, the few tourists who pass pause for a moment, watching and listening to the girl as she plays, tossing in their little mystery coins. She ignores them completely, totally absorbed in her playing.

He remembers her name: Tali. She must be almost eighteen by now. Stefan taught her briefly when he was a student at Brno. She was part of one of the do-gooder university programs for Roma kids, and he was the young, idealistic Stefan. The person he once was, before so many things rained down around him, before playing Vivaldi in Italy for six months of the year dulled any pleasure he'd ever taken in the violin. Before the virus made playing Vivaldi in Italy impossible and left him scrambling for his own crowns and euros once again.

Also before he recognized how little he meant to his girlfriend Nadya, who slept with his best friend in their last year at university. Before he recognized his own limited talent. Before he recognized that all governments lie, that people work themselves to death unthinkingly, that the planet has limited room and limited resources, all of which are being squandered. That only gold has actual value, and yet people are swimming in so much wealth and filthy lucre all around him. Americans, Russians, Brits, Australians, drinking pilsners in Prague, Bellinis in Venice, scoring coke, fucking the locals, barely glancing at the art, barely noticing the talent of a girl like Tali.

He watches the handful of tourists who stop to listen. He knows they have no clue what she's playing—first Dvořák, then the *Ballada* from Janáček's Violin Sonata. Her playing is fluid, tender; there's a youthful freshness to it, a sense of infinite potential, a loss of the self—something he recognizes, even if he's rarely achieved it himself.

A lump forms in his throat as Tali sustains the final, nearly silent note of the *Ballada* for an impossibly long moment. Even there, with the noise of the tram on Wilsonova, bustling pedestrians and traffic all around her, she is somehow in her own private world, a place of perfect, crystalline beauty.

He was maybe twenty when he gave her lessons. She would have been around ten. Even then he recognized her natural talent, realizing that she would completely surpass him one day if she continued to play. He's pleased, and surprised, to see that she has; she had precious little support for her interest in music, he recalls. She'd lived with her grandmother, along with several other siblings, and of course there'd been no money for an instrument. At home she tried to play an old one left behind by one of her uncles, she said. But it had only three strings.

He can't quite see the one she's playing now, it's not recognizable to him, but it has a smooth and rich sound. He wonders, for a moment, how she got it.

He stays to the rear of the crowd who've gathered to listen, not wanting to distract her. Though it looks as if nothing could distract her, nothing could pull her away from the music, from the world she has somehow entered. Her eyes are closed, her chapped lips are parted. She still seems not to comb her jet black hair often, if at all. And yet she has a kind of rarified, saintly beauty. She does not appear to be human.

And then she stuns Stefan, and clearly others—those who were already listening, passersby who suddenly stop, amazed—as she begins to play *Dimineata dup nunta*, "The morning after the wedding," the Gypsy song made famous by Romanian violinist Ion Voicu. It's an overdone piece, in Stefan's opinion, at least in this part of Europe; there are pop music versions that make his teeth ache. It's showy, not really all that difficult to play, but difficult to play well. Difficult to play with the kind of knowing patience of someone like Voicu. But here is Tali, accomplishing that. She plays like Voicu, yet somehow with a softer, gentler touch. Even the weary, impatient Praguers filing in and out of the station stop to listen, to notice how young and slight and unkempt she is, to toss in the occasional 100-crown note.

The instinctive, bleeding-heart reaction to a gypsy girl. He'd been the same, once. Before the hypocrisy of bleeding-hearts like his mother, a government bureaucrat who'd rarely had time for him—except to remind him, always, that she expected more of him—had helped him see the folly in all western governments. All lining up to emulate the United States of America: the most tremendous, teetering folly of them all. Look how absurdly those governments had bungled a global pandemic. A pandemic that recently killed his own bleeding-heart mother.

With her death has come the discovery that she'd left to Stefan a tidy sum, plus her spacious Vinohrady apartment. "One day you'll be glad you were an only child," she used to tell him when he was young and pleaded with her for a brother or sister. At that point, he'd been too young to foresee the inevitable dissolution of her marriage to his distant father.

Presumably this was what she'd had in mind. The strange reality that Stefan may not need to give lessons to bored expat teenagers for Czech crowns or play mind-numbing "beloved classics" in Italian churches for euros again. Which leaves him with the question of what he *will* do now.

When he was a student, when he knew Tali as a little girl, he had thought he might teach. He had an unusual patience with the young players he worked with, even with the ones with no native ability and no particular interest. (That was who he'd been after all, when his mother insisted he begin violin lessons at the age of six.)

But teaching was "soft." Everyone he studied with knew that. His mother, too, had insisted he would be wasting all his years of study and work if he settled into the quiet monotony of teaching. There was an expression in English, his mother told him: *Those who can, do. Those who can't, teach.* Of course teachers were important, she hastened to add; she was superficially appreciative of the helping professions—teachers, nurses and health aides, trash collectors, all of them. Of "essential workers," as they were called now that someone had to deal with all the sick and dying people, which called for a more respectful name, for signs in people's windows thanking them, for New York City residents who banged their pots and pans in gratitude every evening at the same hour.

His mother had held on to that English expression, Stefan supposed, to spite his father. Both of his parents were economists, but his father taught at university, while his mother had done government work. After their divorce, when Stefan was ten, she'd grumbled, frequently, about how little his father earned and contributed to his son's care. How useless his arcane research was, compared to her own real-world endeavors.

It surprised Stefan, how much he'd liked working with children. He'd only signed up for the work to impress Nadya, a voice student who thought he wasn't serious enough, that he didn't care enough about the plight of the world. Which was probably true; he'd mostly cared about playing video games with his friends and getting Nadya into bed. He'd only practiced when he had to.

As it turned out, he was good with the children. Not just the quiet and serious ones, like Tali, even the wild, souped-up little boys, the ones the other student volunteers had struggled to control. He'd been a wild, souped-up little boy himself; he knew how to capture their interest. He drew musical note cartoon characters that blazed trails over keyboards and fretboards; he turned the playing of instruments into video game battles. He'd enjoyed the challenge of getting their attention and then, when he had it, playing for them—lullabies, folk tunes, simple songs that they'd recognize. Soothing them with the music while they played the games he'd created, and in doing so making them curious about the making of those sounds.

"You should teach," his girlfriend said to him one day. "You're so good with the kids." She was one of the organizers of the program—too busy with her vocal training to spend time with the children herself, she insisted, and instead taking credit for running the thing. At the time he'd taken that as a compliment. Now he assumes she was probably insulting him. He shrugs the memory off.

It's true that children interest him. He finds it intriguing, who we are when we start out, compared to who we become. When he sees children he watches them, and he thinks about how a child's face, a child's life, is a blank slate. Until everything starts to happen to them. Until their faces get etched by adulthood, their talent absorbed into the bitter cycle of earning and spending, their natural proclivity for beauty, for art and music, sucked away by other distractions. Until they're swept along like everybody else, caught in the current of an over-tapped river in a dry, dry land.

Three months ago, before he was called back to Prague because of his mother's hospitalization and sudden turn for the worse, he was back in Venice, playing concerts in the church again. One morning, he'd sat drinking an espresso in a bar, staring mindlessly out the front window, when suddenly Charlie was there, walking out of the bookstore across the narrow street and locking the door behind him. There were two children with him, a little boy of maybe four or five and a girl who looked to be a few years older. As Stefan watched, Charlie hoisted the laughing boy onto his shoulders and took the girl's hand, and the three of them headed down the narrow, quiet street. Charlie still walked with the loping assurance of an American who always feels at home—even, Stefan recalls now, when he was sopping wet from a fall into one of Venice's murky canals.

"Hey," he called to the bartender, who looked up from polishing the bar and squinted to see where Stefan was pointing, "isn't that the guy who works at the bookstore?"

"He used to work there," the bartender said, "but it's closed now. The owner died, from the virus. Those are his kids."

For a moment Stefan was confused. "Is he with the owner's wife now?"

The bartender snorted at that. "Are you kidding? Have you seen her? No, no. I hear he's bought the place. She and the kids are moving out of the apartment above the store. He's helping them move, I think."

The next time Stefan saw Charlie he was walking into a bar near the Santa Maria della Pietà church, where Stefan had just finished that night's concert. It was a bar they'd gone to several times two years before, and Stefan followed Charlie inside. He sat down next to him at the bar, nervous about how Charlie might react to seeing him; Stefan had, after all, essentially pushed him into that canal. And though he hadn't quite meant to do it, they *had* been fighting, and seeing Charlie's tall, rangy body flailing in the dark canal had made Stefan feel, momentarily, like he had won.

But when Charlie turned and saw Stefan on the bar stool next to him with his hand stretched out in greeting, he seemed genuinely glad. "Hey man!" he'd exclaimed, clasping Stefan's hand and grasping his shoulder, pulling him in for a brief, manly hug: the confident American male greeting that only someone like Charlie can pull off.

"I'm glad to see you, glad you're back." He pointed to the violin case that Stefan held in his lap. "Are you guys playing at the church again?"

Stefan nodded, slipping off his cloth mask and signaling the bartender for a beer, the same thing Charlie was drinking. "Yes, we're playing the concerts again. The money's still decent, at least for now, but not that many people are coming." He took a sip of his beer and shrugged, smiling at Charlie. "And you know, it's still mostly Vivaldi."

Charlie laughed, nodding. "Oh yeah, I remember," he said and then quoted Stefan from two years before, "The Baroque composer who anticipated climate change: Every season sounds the same."

Stefan smiled, recalling the night he and Charlie met, their free-wheeling conversation about music in this very bar. He started to relax a bit, lowering his violin to the floor at his feet and looking around the bar, which was nearly empty. It was one of the places Charlie knew about, tucked around the corner from the church on a dark, quiet street. The worn wood of the bar and the few small tables glowed in the dim light of flickering lanterns. In the past it would have been packed, mostly with local people—other musicians, students, people who worked in the shops.

He hadn't bought the bookstore, Charlie told Stefan, though he bought most of the stock. Mostly to help Tomasso's wife and their kids, who were moving to Lombardy, to the town where his wife's parents lived. But it was also just a really good collection of books, he said—tons of rare art books, early Italian literature and books on film, first editions in multiple languages. He was shipping most of them to a farm in the U.S. not too far from Philadelphia, to a place his mother had decided to buy. There was a big barn where he could store them for now, though he was going to have to fix it up, get some shelving units, weatherize the place somehow. Tomasso had done a good job with the collection overall, but with all the recent rain and flooding, some of the books had dots of mold. He'd spent weeks sorting and packing them all, cleaning off the mold with hydrogen peroxide, discarding several boxes full that he just couldn't salvage.

"What will you do with them once they're in that barn?" Stefan asked. Surely, he was thinking, you don't plan to live on a farm in the state of Pennsylvania.

"I'm not sure," Charlie said, though he was thinking he might be able to stay interested in selling books, at least for a while. He shrugged. Vivaldi, rare books, both of them seemed to be thinking—what else were you supposed to do after a global pandemic?

"I saw you with the owner's kids one morning last week," Stefan said. "Leaving the bookstore. I asked the bartender if you were with the guy's wife now" He grinned when he said it, assuming they could share the joke.

But "Nah, no, it's not like that," was all Charlie said in response. "I keep an eye on the kids sometimes. Silvia's had a lot of meetings with lawyers and stuff. She's selling the building. That's how they can afford to move."

Something about the innocence of Charlie's response (an innocence that Stefan had always assumed he was faking)—his refusal to claim his due as a man who was so obviously attractive to women, to at least roll his eyes at the suggestion that he might have moved in on some used-up Italian hausfrau—made Stefan grow reckless then, made him venture into dangerous territory. This had always bothered him about Charlie, he recalled, the way he never took the bait, never joined in the joke.

"So are you still pining for your American girl back home? What was her name—Minerva?" Stefan knew full well of course that that was her name. He'd said it with the same exaggerated European pronunciation that night two years ago, when they'd argued and fought at the edge of the Rio di San Luca canal.

He thought he saw a flash of anger in Charlie's eyes then, just for a moment. He liked seeing that, seeing that he could still get a rise out of this guy—and for the first time, he wondered why that mattered to him. But Charlie only nodded and said, "She's not a girl, she's a woman. And yeah, I guess I am still pining for her. We're talking again. It's good actually. But she's way too busy for me right now. So I'm just gonna get busy with these books and see how things go."

He took a long draw on his beer, emptying the glass. "The virus changed her," he said. "It changed everybody."

Stefan tried but failed to persuade Charlie to stay for one more round. He had to get up early, he said. Still a lot of work to do in the store, and he'd promised Tomasso's kids that he'd take them for pizza and a ride on the vaporetto.

He dropped a twenty-euro note on the bar and held out his hand to shake Stefan's one more time. "Good to see you again, man," he said, smiling.

. . .

TALI PERFECTLY EXECUTES the ending of *Dimineata* then reaches down to open her violin case as the crowd that's gathered applauds and whistles. She's smart to end here, with this crowd-pleaser; she's clearly thought this all through.

Had the virus changed him? Stefan wonders as he gets in line to toss some money into Tali's case. He'll give her all the crowns in his pocket, he's decided, plus a few stray euros left from Venice; she'll need to change a lot of euros now.

The virus had taken his mother. That much was different. He was suddenly better off than he'd ever been, than he'd imagined ever being, really. And more alone.

When he looks up after tossing his money into Tali's case, he catches her eye and smiles at her. But it's clear she doesn't recognize him. She gives him a curt nod of thanks. She doesn't return his smile. Maybe the virus has made him unrecognizable, someone with no connection to the twenty-year-old Stefan Tali had once known. He's older, and so is she. She's no longer a child, and he's no longer an idealistic student. He's grown a bit thick in the middle and he's losing his hair. His clothes and glasses are out of fashion, he mistrusts most if not all women, he is bored with his own playing of the violin.

His mother is dead and he lives alone in her apartment, with reminders of her everywhere—the smell of her perfume, her cluttered and messy desk and bookshelves, the bottles of pills in her bathroom. She had been sick for a while, his father told him; her immune system was weak. Something Stefan had not known.

He watches as Tali gathers her money, tenderly places her violin into the case, and then crosses the street to wait for a tram. He wonders where, and how, she is living now. Prague is expensive. He should have given her more, he realizes, but it's too late now. To chase her down and ask if she needs money would probably frighten her.

So instead, he walks to the tram stop, to the side opposite Tali. To take a tram in the other direction, to a nicer part of the city. This is how it works. This is what he's inherited. Comfort, and boredom. Hesitancy. Loneliness.

This is how the world works. He keeps believing that he understands how it could all change for the better. In his idealistic student days, he'd been a socialist, like everyone else he knew. Then he'd morphed into something else, under the influence of new friends he made, musicians, people in bars. The CasaPound people in Italy, though he's come to recognize that a lot of them are idiots.

Maybe he should buy the stock of some struggling bookstore and become a bookman like Charlie; there are bound to be plenty of struggling bookstores in Prague by now. But he'd have no Minerva to wait for while he sorted the books and moved them into his mother's capacious apartment. Only his coins and notes, his mother's statements from the bank, all of it standing in for nothing of any true value. Maybe he should listen to his old school friend Michal, who shows up at his mother's apartment almost every night now with several bottles of beer and tries to convince Stefan to convert all his mother's money to cryptocurrency. Better that, maybe, than these online accounts, these colorful pieces of paper and tokens stamped from cheap metals, more of them minted every minute, coursing around the globe and on the verge of flooding it. Of washing them all away.

Across the track he watches Tali's dark hair, her tattered jeans and sneakers, in the midst of the waiting crowd, until her tram arrives, pauses briefly, and pulls away. And then she and her violin are gone. As if she'd been a ghost, an apparition, a figment of his imagination. Something or someone he'd once known—before adulthood, before Covid—but has lost now, probably for good.

Acknowledgments

Heartfelt thanks to my editor Fred Ramey, for another go-round at Unbridled Books. Fred's writerly sensibility and belief in my work have encouraged and sustained me; he is a writer's dream editor, and I'm so glad our paths first crossed nearly twenty years ago. Thanks also to my agent Emily Williamson, another true writer's friend; I've loved our commiseration and our laughter and look forward to more of both.

Thanks to family and friends for their insightful readings of sections of *The Dime Museum* through the years, especially Gene Garber, Anna Hauser, Jim Hauser, Ruth Knafo Setton, and Virginia Wiles.

I am indebted to my former Moravian College/University colleague Kerry Cheever, Emerita Nursing Professor and Editor of *Brunner & Suddarth's Textbook of Medical-Surgical Nursing*, for several COVID-era conversations about trauma nursing and COVID-19. I won't soon forget the stories she shared from her own experiences as a nurse, and her empathic understanding of the profound loneliness of those early COVID patients.

Also vital to my research:

- Alec Marsh (Professor of English, Muhlenberg College), who shared his work on Ezra Pound's early life and experience at the University of Pennsylvania with me; the scholars, performers, and organizers of the 27th Ezra Pound International Conference ("Ezra Pound, Philadelphia Genius, and Modern

American Poetry"), held at Penn in June 2017; Douglas Wissing's "This Rash Adventure: Ezra Pound at Wabash College" (*The Ryder*, May 28, 2016); Wabash College alumnus Jim Rader's "Hooked on Pound at Wabash" from the *Wabash College Magazine*, July 2008.

- John Anderson, *Art Held Hostage: The Battle over the Barnes Collection* (2003, 2013); Howard Greenfield, *The Devil and Dr. Barnes: Portrait of an American Art Collector* (1987, 2006); *The Art of the Steal* (2009 documentary).

- Ron Devlin's "Wallace Stevens' wife believed to have been model for figure on Mercury dime" (*Reading Eagle*, May 20, 2011), which recounts the work of Berks County historian Patricia Shearer; Milton J. Bates, "Stevens in Love: The Woman Won, the Woman Lost" (*ELH*, Vol. 48, No. 1, Spring 1981); Paul Mariani, *The Whole Harmonium: The Life of Wallace Stevens* (2016).

- Multiple works on aspects of life in nineteenth- and early twentieth-century Chicago, including dime museums and furnished room districts, plus articles on male impersonators of the nineteenth and early twentieth centuries.

Rebecca Makkai writes of "the line between allyship and appropriation" in the Author's Note and Acknowledgments to her novel *The Great Believers*. In creating Maude and Annie and other characters in this book, I hope I've stayed on the right side of that line. I have wished to give voice to the many people who—for reasons of gender, class, sexual orientation, race, disability, and more—have had their own creative stirrings silenced.

Joyce Hinnefeld

About the Author

Joyce Hinnefeld is the author of the short story collections *Tell Me Everything* (winner of the 1997 Bread Loaf Bakeless Prize in Fiction) and *The Beauty of Their Youth*, the novels *In Hovering Flight* and *Stranger Here Below*, and of other short stories and essays. She is an Emerita Professor of English at Moravian University in Bethlehem, PA, director of the Moravian Writers' Conference, and a Program Facilitator with Shining Light, an organization that provides reentry-based programming for incarcerated people throughout the United States.

Find her online at joycehinnefeld.com